Praise for

Swimming Without a Net

"An engaging undersea adventure . . . *Swimming Without a Net* seizes your attention from the very first page. Hang on for a fun-filled ride . . . *Swimming Without a Net* demonstrates why Davidson is considered one of today's premier paranormal authors. I urge everyone to pick up a copy of this entertaining book at your earliest opportunity. This is a not-to-be-missed, laugh-out-loud adventure. Believe me, you will love this story!"
—*Romance Junkies*

"Davidson, the queen of paranormal comedy, has dished up another wickedly funny romp in this follow-up to *Sleeping with the Fishes*."
—*Booklist*

"An entertaining and charming read . . . fast-paced, enjoyable, and at times downright hilarious."   —*Romance Reviews Today*

"A story that will entertain, delight, and enlighten fans of mermaid Fred . . . Fans of Ms. Davidson, rejoice—Fred is back and as sassy as ever!"
—*Fresh Fiction*

"Another wacky, amusing romp from MaryJanice Davidson, the queen of this subgenre. The story line is fast-paced but loaded with humor."   —*Midwest Book Review*

"Wonderful . . . Fred is just as fierce and funny as before . . . Davidson makes Fred and her underwater world seem so natural and real, this is a book you can easily enjoy."

—*Rambles.net*

"This wildly offbeat series has lots of laughs as well as biting social commentary."   —*Romantic Times*

d . . .

D0958725

Fish out of Water

MaryJanice Davidson

JOVE BOOKS, NEW YORK

THE BERKLEY PUBLISHING GROUP
Published by the Penguin Group
Penguin Group (USA) Inc.
375 Hudson Street, New York, New York 10014, USA

Penguin Group (Canada), 90 Eglinton Avenue East, Suite 700, Toronto, Ontario M4P 2Y3, Canada
(a division of Pearson Penguin Canada Inc.)
Penguin Books Ltd., 80 Strand, London WC2R 0RL, England
Penguin Group Ireland, 25 St. Stephen's Green, Dublin 2, Ireland (a division of Penguin Books Ltd.)
Penguin Group (Australia), 250 Camberwell Road, Camberwell, Victoria 3124, Australia
(a division of Pearson Australia Group Pty. Ltd.)
Penguin Books India Pvt. Ltd., 11 Community Centre, Panchsheel Park, New Delhi—110 017, India
Penguin Group (NZ), 67 Apollo Drive, Rosedale, North Shore 0632, New Zealand
(a division of Pearson New Zealand Ltd.)
Penguin Books (South Africa) (Pty.) Ltd., 24 Sturdee Avenue, Rosebank, Johannesburg 2196,
South Africa

Penguin Books Ltd., Registered Offices: 80 Strand, London WC2R 0RL, England

This is a work of fiction. Names, characters, places, and incidents either are the product of the author's imagination or are used fictitiously, and any resemblance to actual persons, living or dead, business establishments, events, or locales is entirely coincidental. The publisher does not have any control over and does not assume any responsibility for author or third party websites or their content.

FISH OUT OF WATER

A Jove Book / published by arrangement with the author

PRINTING HISTORY
Jove mass-market edition / December 2008

ISBN: 978-0-515-14549-6

JOVE®
Jove Books are published by The Berkley Publishing Group,
a division of Penguin Group (USA) Inc.,
375 Hudson Street, New York, New York 10014.
JOVE® is a registered trademark of Penguin Group (USA) Inc.
The "J" design is a trademark belonging to Penguin Group (USA) Inc.

PRINTED IN THE UNITED STATES OF AMERICA

10 9 8 7 6 5 4 3 2 1

For William Alongi: father, grandfather, husband, brother, uncle, friend. Things aren't as exciting without all the grumbling, big guy.

And for Cindy Hwang, who, in the face of enormous personal tragedy, never once lost her kindness, humor, skill, empathy, or professionalism.

As Andrew Vacchs, the finest writer of noir fiction in the twenty-first century and tireless champion of the helpless, once said (and I'm paraphrasing), "If love died with death, this world wouldn't be so hard."

That's just right, sir. That is 100 percent correct.

Acknowledgments

This is the last book of the Fred the mermaid trilogy; the other two are *Sleeping with the Fishes* and *Swimming Without a Net*. (There's also a mermaid novella in my anthology *Dead Over Heels*, which takes place just before the events of this book.)

Although Betsy the vampire queen made me semi-famous (infamous? delusionally famous?), I actually thought up Fred long before I ever wrote *Undead and Unwed*. So it's a little strange to me that I'm putting paid to Fred while Betsy goes on and on and on.

("And on," the critics added snidely, "and on, and on.")

Well, hell. She *is* a vampire. And that's what they do, I s'pose. Fred, however, is mortal.

Anyway, I wanted to thank Cindy Hwang, my editor, for going along with my idea for a grumpy mermaid, and for never asking, "What, exactly, is wrong with you?" At least, not out loud.

My agent, Ethan Ellenberg, for making the deal happen.

Leis Pederson, who catches many of my boneheaded mistakes and never gets the credit.

Acknowledgments

My Yahoo! group, for their support.

Charlaine Harris and her fan group, three of whom dressed as Fred, Dr. Bimm, and Jonas for the *Romantic Times* 2008 convention, forcing me to pretend my eyes were leaking because of allergies.

And, always, my friends and family, for tirelessly listening to my near-constant bitching.

MaryJanice Davidson
www.maryjanicedavidson.net

Author's Note

Although there is a Florida Aquarium, I have no idea if it's open at the top or if it's possible for people to fall into Shark Bay. It's quite possible (more like probable) I took some liberties. Sorry, Florida Aquarium.

Also, although there are many fine naval bases in Florida (in the country, actually), the Sanibel Station is 100 percent made up, as were the actions of the sailors stationed there. Got that? Fiction. Not true. Please don't ask me why I hate America, okay?

Also, salmon pink bridesmaid gowns do clash terribly with green hair.

Fish out
of Water

I love treason but hate a traitor.

—JULIUS CAESAR

It's silly to go on pretending that under the skin we are all brothers. The truth is more likely that under the skin we are all cannibals, assassins, traitors, liars, hypocrites, poltroons.

—HENRY MILLER

A mermaid's not a human thing
An' courtin' sich is folly;
Of flesh an' blood I'd rather sing,
What ain't so melancholy.

— E. J. BRADY, "Lost and Given Over"

A reporter meets interesting people. If he endures, he will get to know princes and presidents, popes and paupers, prostitutes and panderers.

—JIM BISHOP

Time magazine: "Is it true that if you help a mermaid, you get one wish?"
Fredrika Bimm: "Shut up."

Fuck the fathers. They should know better.

— PAT CONROY, *The Prince of Tides*

The Story So Far

Fredrika Bimm is a hybrid—her father was a merman who got her hippie mother pregnant one night on the beach and then disappeared forever. Part of both worlds and feeling out of place pretty much everywhere, Fred's dearest wish is to keep herself to herself and stay under everyone's radar.

Circumstances, however, make that impossible. In the last year and a half, she has helped Prince Artur of the Undersea Folk (what the mer-people call themselves) figure out who was dumping toxins into Boston Harbor, fallen for a fellow marine biologist (Dr. Thomas Pearson, who writes romance novels on the side), fought pirates (yes, pirates), attended a Pelagic (don't ask), met the king of the Undersea Folk (who is obsessed with the HBO series *Deadwood*), walked in on her mother and stepfather having sex, walked in on her boss (Dr. Barb) and her best friend (Jonas) doing their impersonation of the Thing That Can't Stop Kissing, visited the Cayman Islands, and watched as several of her father's people showed themselves (tails and all) to the world.

Also, she's taken a leave of absence from her job at the New England Aquarium. So, she's been busy.

Now, six months after the first of the Undersea Folk were seen on CNN, the world is transfixed by the idea that mermaids are real . . . have always been real . . . and there could be one living right next door.

Also, she has to house hunt in Florida. During tourist season.

Oh, the humanity.

Prologue

He stared, transfixed. His people were showing themselves to the world! How could the royal family— the *king*—go along with this? It went against centuries of tradition and ingrained behavior.

He instantly started figuring how he could turn the situation to his advantage.

One

🦭

"Excuse me, but are you a mermaid?"

"Why?" Fred was poking through the large, airy kitchen and trying not to show how impressed she was with the ocean view. She knew the Realtor would pick up on it like a bloodhound to sweat. "Do I get a discount? 'Show us your fin and we'll show you ten percent off.' Like that?"

The Realtor colored, which, given that she had the creamy complexion natural to most redheads, gave the impression that she was about to have a stroke. Fred wondered how long it would take for the paramedics to show.

"I didn't mean anything by it." She coughed. "It's just—your hair."

"I know, don't tell me. I fired my stylist." Fred fussed with the ends of her green hair, which were now chin-length as opposed to tumbling halfway down her back. Much easier to take care of, though her friend Jonas had shrieked like he'd been stabbed when he'd seen it. "And I'm still getting grief about it from my friend. My stupid, irritating friend."

"But it's blue."

"Technically it's green." She opened a cupboard to see how deep it was. "You know how the ocean looks blue but it's really green? Same with my— Does the garbage disposal work?"

"Wha— Yes. And the house comes with all the appliances, as well as lawn maintenance. So are you?"

"I dunno. It's pretty expensive. And what do I need four bedrooms for? You know what that'll mean for me? Drop-in guests. 'Say, Fred, you've got plenty of room, we're staying here for a month.' Any idea how much I hate drop-ins? I hate them like a fat kid hates Slim-Fast.

Besides, I live in a Boston apartment most of the year. Mowing a lawn would actually be a treat for me."

"No, I meant, are you a mermaid?"

"The term is Undersea Folk."

"Yes, are you?" The Realtor was actually leaning toward Fred with the urgency of her question. Fred found she was backed up against the dishwasher, close enough to count the threads in the buttons on the Realtor's blouse. "Because I know I've seen you on TV. On the news. I'm sure of it. So are you?"

"Why, are you afraid you won't be able to track down all my references?" Fred sidled away from her and walked through the dining area.

This entire side of the house had enormous windows, all of which boasted ocean views of the Gulf side. It was 2:30 p.m. on Sanibel Island, Florida, February 11, and she was walking around inside a house that would sell painlessly for five million dollars, even with the housing market deep in the shitter as it was. The Realtor was asking five thousand a week to rent it out.

"Also, you swam in from the ocean side. Most people drive to the house."

"Is this your not-too-subtle way of bitching about

me tracking salt water all over the floors? Besides, I had to work off the brownie sundae I had for breakfast. What about the washer and dryer?"

"Right through here." The Realtor, whose name Fred had forgotten, opened a door off the kitchen and gestured. Fred peeked around the corner and observed a full-sized washer/dryer combo in a spotlessly clean laundry room.

"Hmmm."

The entire first floor (except for the bathroom) was one gigantic room, the front hall leading to the dining area leading to the kitchen leading to the living room leading to a large porch that ran nearly the length of the house. The walls were the color of Coffee-Mate; the furniture and décor were done in Modern Millionaire. All the windows were thrown wide and a fresh breeze made the curtains billow.

Upstairs were several bedrooms and three more bathrooms, one with a Jacuzzi big enough for a soccer team. Two of the bedrooms boasted ocean views as well. The cream-colored walls made the large house appear even more spacious.

Fred stared thoughtfully out over the lawn, eyeing the

outdoor Jacuzzi and swimming pool. Her boyfriend/ suitor/someday-sovereign, Prince Artur, had encouraged this move. And she had to admit, it wasn't the worst idea she'd ever heard.

Ever since Undersea Folk had started coming out of the water closet (heh), she'd been fielding interviews and handling the press and in general acting as go-between for the royal family, the Undersea Folk, and surface dwellers. As a result, the world was assuming the Undersea Folk's primary residence was here, just off the coast of Sanibel Island.

They were wrong.

Which suited the king just fine.

But Fred craved her own space to retreat to, and never mind Artur's argument that she could use the ocean as an escape hatch. The ocean—yech! Seaweed and barracudas and mouthy fish (mouthy telepathic fish, anyway) and silt and frankly, she vastly preferred a pool to the large, messy ocean.

Yes, she needed her own space and perhaps this zillion-dollar mansion was it. Although her stepfather was wealthy, he hadn't flaunted it when she was a kid, and although she had a healthy trust fund, she'd always been content with her little one-bedroom apartment in Boston.

This place, though . . . Artur had pointed out that, as the girlfriend of the prince, she needed more than a teeny Boston apartment. How had he put it? *Someplace worthy of our future queen.* Amazing she even remembered what he'd said, she'd been laughing so hard.

"I dunno," she said. "It's really big. And—"

The front door boomed open and there stood Prince Artur, well over six feet, with shoulder-length hair the color of smashed rubies, and eyes almost the same shade. He hadn't shaved for a couple of weeks and his beard was also a deep red. His shoulders were so broad, and he was so tall, he barely fit in the doorway. He was shirtless, and barefoot, and clad only in a pair of denim shorts.

"Ho, Little Rika! Is the cottage to your liking?" He frowned, glancing around. "It looked more fitting from the outside."

Fred smirked at the gaping Realtor. "Now, him? *He's* a mermaid. So to speak."

Two

🦭

"I was told this would be a suitable residence for my little Rika," Prince Artur said with a frown.

"It's plenty suitable; don't be such a royal snob."

"I do not think it is fitting for one who will one day be queen," Artur persisted with maddening stubbornness.

That did it. "I'll take it," Fred told the astonished Realtor, who was staring at the prince as if she were in some sort of sex trance. "And I'll pay asking and all the fees and sign whatever I need to sign, but I need to move in by the end of the week. Open-ended lease, six-month minimum, whatever security deposit you need. Okay?"

"Neh," the Realtor said.

"Great. And quit that 'one day will be queen' talk, Artur, I've told you before. Just because I'm with you doesn't mean I'm—you know. With you." *Which, technically, makes me a tease. Hmm. Not sure I care for—*

"Ah, Little Rika." Artur snatched at her but she managed to dodge out of the way, nearly braining herself on the cupboard she'd left open. "One day you will see the wisdom of our love match."

"And don't call me that. It's Fred. Or Fredrika. Or Dr. Bimm. Or Bitchcakes. Or—"

"I've seen you on TV, too!" the Realtor exclaimed. "You're the prince of all the mermaids!"

"Undersea Folk," Artur and Fred said in unison.

"You look just like your dad!"

Artur inclined his head, the closest thing to a bow he bothered with. "That is my honor, good lady, and you are kind to point it out."

"Vomit, vomit, vomit," Fred mumbled.

"Let's see, you were on CNN . . . and *People* did

9

that big cover story on you guys . . ." The Realtor snapped her fingers and pointed at Fred. "I knew you looked familiar. The hair threw me—it was longer in the pictures."

"Congrats, Nancy Drew. Why don't you scamper on back to the clubhouse and draw up my damned contract?"

"Forgive the lady," Artur said, gallantly offering the dazzled Realtor his elbow and walking her to the door. "She has been seeking a temporary home on land for many days and it has left her in ill humor."

"Being saddled with a stupid nickname has left me in a worse humor!" Fred bawled after him.

"More so than usual, though the thought makes me tremble," he added in a mutter. "How kind you were to show her this small and charming cottage; we are sure you will be as efficient in the rest of our business dealings."

"Yeah, thanks a heap," Fred called. "Bye."

"Oh. Oh! Yes, of course. Good-bye! Oh. But I can't leave you here, since technically this isn't—"

"The lady and I will be leaving as well."

"Oh. You're going to jump back in the ocean, aren't you?"

"It's quicker than calling a cab," Fred said, taking a last look around her new home before following Artur out the back door.

Three

🦐

Fred stripped out of her shorts, T-shirt, and panties and left them on the lawn. What the hell . . . in a few days this was going to be her home, anyway. She wondered who had left the clothes for her on the lawn in the first place—it's not like she could swim with a tail in a pair of shorts. One of Artur's crew, probably.

She shouldn't have been surprised that he'd be underwhelmed by the house—he was used to enormous underwater palaces. When the Undersea Folk built something, they thought big. And why not? Wasn't most of the planet covered with water? They were used to having three-quarters of the planet to spread out in.

There was no beach leading to the Gulf; instead there was a sharp drop-off and a long dock. She trotted to the end of the dock, cast an amused glance at the shit-caked plastic owls perched on the pier, and dove off, shifting immediately to her tail form. Artur was several feet ahead of her, effortlessly moving through the water with powerful thrusts of his tail.

As a hybrid, her tail wasn't as long as his, nor as wide, nor as beautifully colored. Artur's reminded her of a peacock's, all greens and blues, while hers seemed less magnificent, almost dull. *Be grateful you have a tail at all,* she reminded herself. She might have taken after her human mother, after all, and not have been able to shift. Bad enough she couldn't swim in her legs . . . imagine not being able to breathe underwater.

She caught up with him after a few more strokes, glaring at a barracuda that was swimming annoyingly close. The fish sneered at her and darted away, the predator's thoughts

(big thing can't bite the big thing hungry not big thing)

setting up an echo in her mind.

Hey, Artur.

Yes, my dear one?

I gotta say, it was pretty smart of your dad to let the world think your HQ is here.

HQ?

Headquarters. The seat of the government, or power, or the capital—everyone thinks it's here instead of the Black Sea.

He flipped over and floated on his back, a good thirty feet beneath the waves. She swam beneath him and then over him, waiting for his response.

It will take some time before we can completely trust your mother's people, Little Rika. I hope this gives you no offense.

Offense? Who warned you about them in the first place? Hmm, lemme think—oh yeah! It was me. You know how many people have been fucked over in the name of scientific advancement? It's pretty damned smart, actually, letting the world think we all hang out here. But one thing your dad's got to spare is brain-power.

Artur laughed in her head. *So true, my Rika!*

14

They passed two more Undersea Folk—a man and a woman, the man with hair the color of daffodils; the woman with hair so pure a black it seemed to swallow up the light.

Greetings, my prince.

Ho, Prince Artur! Fredrika.

Fred nodded to them both. It didn't escape her notice that only one had acknowledged her and called her by name, though she knew damn well she was notorious enough that all the Undersea Folk knew her on sight.

Notorious.

Shit.

She was somewhat mystified that it bugged her—she'd never been one to sweat what strangers thought. But dammit, the Undersea Folk who didn't like her didn't know her. They didn't like her because Dear Old Dad had been a traitor. Big believers in the whole "the guppy doesn't fall far from the frog" school of thought.

And dammit, it wasn't *fair*. It was fine if someone didn't like her based on her own merits—and the list was long and distinguished, both of her odious faults and the people who didn't like her—but they ought to

15

at least get to know her before they decided she was a shit.

I know your thoughts, my Rika. Shall I thrash the one who dared ignore you?

Don't make it worse. It's no big deal.

Ah, Little Rika. Your lady mother did not teach you to lie. How unusual for a surface dweller, even one as noble as your mother.

Fred had no answer to that.

Four

She spilled her tea when the front door was thrown open. More mermaids? Her stepfather? Another guy who wanted to shoot her for profit? *Time? Newsweek? People?*

"Dum dum dah dum!" Jonas cried, arms spread, suitcases at his feet. "Dum *dum* dah dum!"

"Something nutball this way comes," Fred muttered, dabbing the tea off her shorts and slowly getting up from the couch.

It was moving day and she had been in the house less

than three hours. She cursed the impulse she'd followed last week to (a) give her best friend her new address and (b) send him a spare key. Stupid force of habit. He'd had spare keys to her homes for years.

Did this mean on a subconscious level she actually *wanted* him to show up in her life?

Stupid subconscious.

"Ooooh, nice digs," Jonas said, lugging his suitcases inside, listing radically to the left under the weight of the two in his hand. "Are you finally going to live in the manner to which your stepfather and hot mom are accustomed?"

"Shut up," she said automatically, but, as she'd known, he wasn't deterred.

He was an exhaustingly cheerful blond, taller than she—about six-three—with the mind of an engineer (he designed shampoo for the Aveda corporation) and a black belt in aikido. He was also the most metrosexual guy on the planet—continually being mistaken for gay (mostly because he insisted on drinking appletinis)— and a loyal friend.

They had been best friends since the second grade.

"So, check it," he said, kicking one of his suitcases

out of the way and crossing the room to plop down on the chair opposite Fred. "Barb has given me carte blanche to plan our wedding."

"Barf," she muttered.

"Because, as you know, she's been through this before."

Fred knew. Dr. Barb, her boss at the New England Aquarium, had been married to a real shitheel several years ago.

"And I've decided, since you're stuck down here playing go-between for Artur's folks and us lowly humans—"

"To burst in on me and make me spill my tea?"

"—to have the wedding here. On Sanibel Island."

Fred tried not to, but she couldn't help it: she groaned.

"Aw." Jonas beamed. "I knew you'd be pleased." He propped his sandaled feet up on the coffee table, admiring his no-polish pedicure for a moment. "So as my best man, so to speak—"

Fred groaned again. "Don't you think I've got enough on my plate right now?"

"Oh, who cares. Also, I bring a message from my

blushing bride-to-be, who wanted me to remind you that she's still refusing your resignation."

"For God's sake," Fred said crossly. "I haven't set foot in the aquarium for ages."

"Hey, don't shoot the messenger, doll."

"I'd like to *throttle* the messenger."

"Barb says you're the best marine biologist she's ever hired. Also, since you outed yourself to her as a mermaid, there's no way in hell she's letting you quit." He yawned. "So which room should I take?"

"And so it begins," she muttered. "I told her. I told that Realtor. Drop-ins. I hate drop-ins."

"Anyway," Jonas said, well used to ignoring her bitching, "I'd like the wedding to take place on a private beach, so I'll need your help with that, and also with other wedding minutiae. Can you clear your calendar this week to help me with cake tasting? Also, you'll need to buy a ridiculously classy and expensive bridesmaid dress—unless you want to get a tux instead."

"Can't you just whip out a gun and shoot me in the face?"

"Maybe tomorrow," he said comfortingly.

Five

Fred was trying hard not to glare at the reporter from *Time* and having her usual degree of success. For the hundredth time, she questioned the king's wisdom in making her the go-between between surface dwellers and Undersea Folk. The king's argument—that she was the only half-and-half on the planet—had seemed so logical at the time . . . Clearly he had paid no attention to her poor interpersonal skills.

"Several countries are offering citizenship to the mermaids—"

"Undersea Folk."

"—how do you feel about that?"

"I feel they don't need land citizenship. They've got the run of the oceans. I also think it's typical of humans to assume Undersea Folk would jump at the chance for U.S. citizenship. Because that's where you're going, right? It's not altruistic in any way. America wants dibs on the finned."

The reporter, a slender, balding man with warm brown eyes, smiled. "Interesting point."

"Insulting point, actually. But have it your way."

"So tell me about yourself—your mother's human, and your father—"

"Next question."

The reporter blinked. "I understand that some of the Undersea Folk don't care for you because your father—"

"Next question."

"Is it true that if you help a mermaid, you get a wish?"

She stared at him. He chuckled nervously under her gaze and added, "Or have I been watching too many movies?"

"It's not true. If you help a mermaid, I get to punch you in the teeth. That's the rule."

"You're an, ah, unusual diplomat."

"Take that back!"

"All right, all right, you're a lousy diplomat."

"Thanks," she said, mollified, thinking: *How did I end up here? Now? Doing this job? With these people?*

"So would you say the Undersea Folk are less—ah—warlike than humans?"

"Less warlike?" she asked blankly.

"There's been some talk about the comparisons, and several Undersea Folk have made no secret of the fact that they don't trust—what do they call us? Surface dwellers?"

"Can you blame them?"

"So you're not denying it?"

She stifled a sigh. More Homo sapiens arrogance. *They're not like us, but we'll find a peg to jam them into anyway.* Ugh.

"Undersea Folk are like anyone else. There are saints, there are assholes, but most of them are somewhere in between. Like anyone else on the planet, you need to get to know one before you decide what kind of person they are. And like anyone else on the planet, you can't say every member of the species acts or talks or thinks the same." Duh. For a moment she'd thought she'd said it out loud. What she *had* said out loud was probably bad enough.

"Oh, this is dynamite," the reporter enthused. "Do you mind if I change 'assholes' to 'jerks'?"

"Censorship," she observed. "Alive and well in the home of the free."

Thick-skinned, like most journalists, he ignored that. "And we'll be sending a photographer over to take your picture—say, two o'clock?"

Fred grimaced, which the reporter took as a strained smile of acquiescence.

"And say, how about a demonstration? Can you—I mean, we see the mer—the Undersea Folk with their tails, or with legs, but nobody's ever seen them shift form. Maybe you could—"

"Do I *look* like a performing seal?"

"So, no." He slapped his notebook shut. "Well, thanks for your time, Dr. Bimm."

She grunted.

"Say, could I get your autograph for my little girl? She's crazy about mermaids."

Oh, Lord, this is punishment for all my sins.

Six

She was resting on the bottom of the pool when she saw Jonas appear, squatting beside the deep end. He looked wavy yet distinct, and he was wearing a pair of shorts so orange they hurt her eyes. He was gesturing impatiently to her.

She ignored him.

His gestures became more urgent.

She yawned and stretched her arms out over her head, a lazy flick of her tail propelling her halfway to the shallow end.

Now he was pointing both middle fingers at her, jabbing the air. She snorted, a stream of bubbles popping to the surface.

He leapt in, swam busily for a moment, then tried to grab her arm and haul her to the surface.

Oh, pal. Mistake.

Jonas must be really agitated, or he'd have remembered she was three times stronger and faster. She wriggled easily from his grip, spun him around, grabbed his ankle, and propelled him through the water with a healthy shove. He nearly brained himself on the steps leading into the shallow end, then bobbed halfway to the surface.

In fact, maybe he *did* brain himself, because he was floating facedown in the water.

Don't fall for that one again.

He still wasn't moving.

He gets you every time with this one.

Maybe she'd pushed it a little far with the roughhousing.

Moron!

She agreed with her self-assessment, but nonetheless reached him in half a second, seized him by the shirt, and flipped him over. They both bobbed to the surface.

He opened his eyes and spat a stream of water at her forehead. "We were supposed to be at the caterer's ten minutes ago."

She let go of him in disgust and wiped her face. "Must have slipped my mind."

"Sure. Now get your fishy butt out of this pool, get dressed, and haul ass to the car."

"You don't need me," she whined. "You're way better at this stuff than I am."

"We're the Team Supreme, dumbass. Now get going."

"Shouldn't you be shielding your eyes at the sight of my breathtaking nudeness?"

"Oh, like I haven't seen your knockers every week since the second grade."

She giggled in spite of herself. "I'm pretty sure I didn't *have* knockers in the—"

"Out. Dress. Car. Caterer."

"You know, I'm under a lot of pressure," she

27

grumbled, shifting from tail to legs and stomping up the shallow end steps to the patio. "I don't need to take shit from Groomzilla."

"You'll be taking a smack in the mouth from Groomzilla if you don't haul ass. Tail. Whatever."

She laughed at him; she couldn't help it. Jonas was never more hilarious than when he was pretending to be a badass.

Seven

§

"Well, how about this one?"

"If I have to jam one more piece of cake down my gullet, I'm going to vomit all over your baker."

The baker, a cadaverously scrawny fellow Fred distrusted on sight (Did he never sample his own product? Why wasn't there an ounce of fat on him?), grimaced but hauled out more slices on napkins.

They were seated practically *in* the front window at a small table set for two. A small, romantic table: silver candlesticks, snow-colored linen napkins, real china. Jonas, of course, was loving it. Fred, not so much.

"This is one of my favorites," the baker said with quiet insistence.

"I can't."

Jonas remained undaunted and said, between chomps, "But it's chocolate!"

Fred moaned. Chocolate with ganache filling. Vanilla sponge cake with raspberry filling. Carrot cake—blurgh! German cake with coconut cream filling. Strawberry cake with strawberry jam filling. Lemon chiffon with Meyer lemon curd filling. Angel food cake with no filling. Angel food cake with coconut filling. Red velvet cake with vanilla buttercream filling. Coconut cake with chocolate fondant. Marble cake with chocolate buttercream frosting. Orange cake with (yurgh!) marmalade filling. Orange poppy seed (double yurgh!) with no filling. Banana cake with coconut filling. Spice cake with (vomit) lemon poppy seed filling. Mocha cake with coffee buttercream filling.

"I can't," she said again, positive she'd put on five pounds in the last half hour.

"Well, *I* can't decide between the lemon chiffon, the mocha, or the vanilla sponge cake." Jonas chomped busily, then said, spraying the spotless tablecloth with crumbs, "Nope. Too rich."

"Have all three, then," she said crossly.

"We're not *all* made of money, Madame Grouchy-pants," he sniffed, unaware that he looked ridiculous with frosting on his chin.

"Jesus, *I'll* pay for them, okay? Just pick. I'll write you a check for ten grand right now if I can just leave."

"You're supposed to help me pick. That's why you're here."

"And I thought I was here to clog my arteries and flop facedown into buttercream frosting during my heart attack."

"We also have apple," the scrawny baker added.

"Twenty grand," Fred begged. "Anything. My checkbook's right here."

"Oh, all right, you can buy the cakes. But we still have to go see the caterer."

"I *can't*," she cried. "You're not listening: I will vomit. Puke. Yark. Blurgh. Spew. Shout at the floor.

31

Whatever. I'll do it. I'm so close to tilt right now, I could be a Vegas slot machine. I—"

"Say," Skinny Baker said, "haven't I seen you on TV?"

She fled.

Eight

🐟

Then—then! Not only is my best friend (and worst enemy) marrying my boss, the wedding's happening here. On Sanibel. And I have to help him pick out cakes and food and tuxes and flowers. All because he's so hot to get hitched the damned wedding's happening in two months. Two! Months! Like I don't have enough things to worry about!

You have many trials, Little Rika.

Artur's tone sounded right—sympathetic and warm—but he was having a terrible time hiding his smile. Much more so than, say, the average human: Artur had the typical dentition of full-blooded Undersea Folk, and had teeth to rival a great white.

They were a few miles out into the Gulf, swimming about thirty feet below the surface. Although Fred normally wasn't a fan of ocean swimming, she couldn't fault the more-or-less beautiful waters of the Gulf of Mexico. You just had to avoid the areas her mother's people had cheerfully polluted the hell out of. And ignore the sneers of the occasional passing nurse shark.

She had fled the bakery and, since Jonas had driven, ran to the first beach she could find—and on Sanibel, they were plentiful. She was out of her clothes in seconds (how many outfits had she left scattered on various beaches around the world?) and into the water, flailing helplessly until she switched to her tail. Then she'd arrowed beneath the waves and put major distance between her and the shore, as quickly as she could.

The irony: if she was home, if she was in Boston, she would have retreated to her tiny apartment and barred the door for a week. But her rental down here was too big, too open, and didn't feel like hers. She was too easily tracked down in the swimming pool. And here, in the ocean, she chanced running into Undersea Folk who hated her because of what her father had done before she was conceived, never mind born.

I am the unluckiest hybrid on the planet.

Oh, stop it, she scolded herself, zipping past a school of snook that were busy trying to stay the hell out of her way. Their panicked thoughts raced across her brain like confetti: *big one eat no eat do not eat no big one no eat!*

Knock it off, she sent back. *I'm stuffed; you don't have to worry about a thing.*

First off, she was the only hybrid on the planet (probably). Second, zillions had it worse. No money. No idea where their next meal was coming from. No way to breathe underwater without scuba gear. Next, she was at the top of the food chain—on both her mother's *and* her father's side. Unlike, say, anything else that swam in the ocean.

And finally, nobody twisted her arm to do any of this crap. She wasn't a victim—far from it. She could have said no. It's not like she didn't know how.

Then why do I feel like everything's spinning out of my control?

Well. There was the small fact that two years ago, only a handful of people knew she grew a tail when she swam. Two years ago, her love life was not at all complicated. (Nonexistent would be the more accurate term.) Jonas wasn't dating Dr. Barb. The world of surface dwellers had no idea mermaids (as they insisted on referring to her father's people) existed. Oh, and thousands of Undersea Folk hadn't decided to hate her because of her shitheel dad.

I prob'ly just need a nap.

She darted past a few goliath grouper, slowing to watch them—she'd never seen that particular species outside an aquarium. She knew it was illegal to keep them if you caught them—the rule down here for goliath grouper was strictly catch and release. Pity. She'd heard grouper were delicious.

She was so absorbed in indulging her inner science geek she didn't see the two Undersea Folk until they were swimming right above her.

Hi, she sent cautiously.

Hello, one of them sent back. It was a male, with a tail much longer, broader, and prettier than hers, all peacock blues and greens. His hair was also green, the color of mashed peridots; his eyes exactly matched. His shoulders were broad, tapering to a narrow waist, and she realized yet again that male Undersea Folk had no chest hair.

Did they shave, the better to be more aerodynamic? Naw. Just something else that set them apart from surface dwellers.

Hello, Fredrika Bimm, the other one said, a female with a narrow, bright yellow tail. Her hair floated around her in a cloud—a literal cloud, as it was perfectly white. *Are you well?*

Hallelujah. Undersea Folk who were going to wait to get to know her before hating her.

As can be expected, I s'pose, she replied. The three of them circled one another. *I didn't catch your names.*

I am Keekenn, the male said, *and this is my mate, Rashel.*

Rochelle, Rochelle, Fred thought inanely. A young girl's strange erotic journey from Milan to Minsk.

I've got to stop watching all those Seinfeld *reruns.*

What? Rashel asked.

Nothing, Fred sent back hastily. *Thinking about something else. Do you guys live around here?*

Not at all. Our home is off the coast of Greenland. We came down here to show numbers to His Majesty the king.

Ah! The better to fool you with, my dear.

Pardon? Keekenn asked.

You know. So the surface dwellers think you guys mostly live here. As opposed to being all over the world, and/or the Black Sea.

I have never seen a surface dweller up close before, Rashel admitted, arching her arms over her head and zipping past Fred. There was a spray of blood and scales, and then the woman was chomping on the head of a grouper and offering the body to her mate. Fred, who was allergic to fish, managed not to vomit and pawed the scales away from her face. *I am most curious. Perhaps it will be an agreeable experience.*

They're not all bad, Fred agreed.

Forgive my mate, she is in pup. Would you like some?

Fred's hand shot up and she pinched her lips together to forestall the barf reflex. *No, no, I've already eaten. You guys knock yourselves out.* In pup? What the hell did that mean? Pregnant?

Hmm. Her inner science geek surged forward with a hundred questions and Fred ruthlessly stomped it. She debated mentioning that it was illegal to devour grouper, then decided that surface dweller fishing rules probably didn't apply to your average pregnant mermaid.

I don't s'pose you guys know where Artur is?

The two exchanged glances, and when Rashel answered it was quite cautiously: *He is several miles from here, in meet with the king. Can you not call him?*

This wasn't the time to explain that, as a half-and-half, her underwater telepathy was quite limited. Her range was poor, to be perfectly blunt. And out of the water, unlike pure-blooded Undersea Folk, she had no telepathy at all. That had been difficult for Artur to get used to. Apparently, it made her borderline retarded in the eyes of many of her father's people. Hurdle number twenty-nine to vault before things ran smoothly.

I didn't want to bother them, she lied.

We did run into another friend of yours, Rashel added.

Oh, yeah?

Indeed. We must be going, but you will see her very soon. It was agreeable to meet you.

Likewise. Her? What friend would they know of who was a *her?*

Rashel and her husband swam away—not one for long good-byes were the Undersea Folk—leaving Fred momentarily alone. The presence of three predators had cleared the area of every single fish, and even a couple of sharks. She had no idea what to—

Ho, Fredrika Bimm!

She spun. And gaped. *Tennian?*

Of course, her blue-haired rival replied, sounding pleased. *Perhaps you were expecting my irritating brother?*

No. That, Fred didn't need.

Rival? Where had *that* come from?

But Fred, a lousy liar, was even worse at lying to herself, and she knew perfectly well where that had come from.

40

Nine

Tennian, cousin to Prince Artur and girlfriend of Dr. Thomas Pearson, swam close and squeezed Fred's arm in what she probably thought was a warm greeting, but which actually made Fred's arm go instantly numb.

How nice to see you again, Fredrika! I had hoped to run over you.

Into me. And that's super. I s'pose Thomas is around here somewhere. It took a great deal of effort to sound casual and not terribly interested in the answer.

Tennian shrugged. *Very likely. You will see him soon, I am sure.*

Great.

Is it not marvelous in these seas? So warm, and such life! Too many boats, though, she added thoughtfully, looking up as a fleet of Jet Skis went by fifteen feet above their heads.

Tourist season, Fred explained. *So you guys came down to answer the king's call?* As soon as she asked, she realized what a dumb question it was. The king didn't have to call. Tennian was by far the most curious mermaid Fred had ever met, and the girl was absolutely fascinated with surface dwellers. If there was a gathering, a meeting, a boat full of tourists hoping to catch sight of a mermaid, a press conference, a pirate ship, a—a Tupperware party, Tennian was there.

She was a striking woman—annoyingly, all the purebred Undersea Folk were easy on the eyes, not a pimple or cross-eyed mutant in the bunch—with dark blue hair and eyes that were even darker, the way small sapphires sometimes looked black.

When the Undersea Folk showed themselves to the surface for the first time, Tennian had been shot.

It hadn't done a thing to squash her curiosity.

And that had been, of course, when Dr. Thomas Pearson, that cheating shallow wretch, had fallen for her. And off they'd gone into the wild blue yonder . . . or wherever a mermaid and a human went to bang their brains out.

Cheating? That wasn't fair, she had to admit. It's not like she'd told him she'd loved him. It's not like they had ever even dated. *He'd* been the one to say he wanted to stick around. And then left for a year.

To finish his fellowship, her conscience reminded her. *Not to abandon you.*

Never mind that. It wasn't the leaving. No, what stung was how quickly Thomas had shifted allegiance. He'd thought she was the bee's knees, but Fred should have kept in mind Thomas had become a marine biologist *because* he was a mermaid freak. He'd been perfectly happy to go off with Tennian and leave Fred yet *again . . .*

Oh, quit it.

What? Tennian asked, her dark blue hair floating around her as she peered, in vain, for something to catch and devour. Girl had a healthy appetite, among other things.

Never mind. So how've you been? All healed up, I guess?

Indeed. Thomas tended me quite well.

Oh, I have no fucking doubt about that.

And here you are, Fred sent politely.

Yes, yes! Already today I have spoken to a man from the land of Texas, two women on their way to 'bridge,' although whether that is a noun or a verb I cannot say, and six children who swam out when they saw me just off their beach.

Just be careful. You don't want to get shot again.

No, I do not! But they were all very nice. I have also seen you on the television machine many times.

Don't remind me.

The king was wise to appoint you our representative.

That's open for debate. Speaking of royalty, you seen your cousin around?

Oh, yes. Unlike some others, Tennian didn't hold Fred's poor range telepathy against her. Tennian didn't hold anything against her. It made her awfully hard to dislike, even if she was boning Thomas. *He comes now—shall I call him for you?*

That'd be great.

Dammit. The girl was just too nice. Dammit!

Ten

So Artur had come darting through the water toward her and Tennian had gone off somewhere and they'd swum together and she'd bitched about her morning. She was careful not to mention Thomas was back in town; Artur made no secret that he thought of the man as the one rival for Fred's affection.

It seems your mating rituals are grueling to the extreme, he teased, and she laughed in spite of herself.

No, anything Jonas is involved with is grueling to the extreme. You'd think I'd be used to it by now.

You would think.

Oh, and I met with that reporter from Time.

Ah, thank you. I have no liking for your press and nor does my good father the king. It is best left to those who understand them.

Fred snorted.

I know that sound! You think my father has chosen wrong. You always think, when complimented, that the other is wrong.

Fred had to admit the redheaded SOB understood her pretty well. It was as irritating as it was flattering.

I just wish it was over with, you know? The wedding. All the press junk. I wish we could go back to our lives.

So do all who are called to greatness, Little Rika.

Called to greatness! she shrieked in his head, giggling like a madwoman. *Oh! That's too good, Artur! That's too damned funny!*

He seized her by the hands, surprising her into choking off her laughter. He was gazing down at her with his intense, ruby gaze. His chest was so broad it filled her world; his face, so handsome and intent, filled her heart. Or someplace lower.

Little Rika, it has been my honor to have you at my side these many months. You have done—as I knew you would—great things for my people. You have given up much to be our liaison. And I have watched you with great pride. But I must press for a more formal arrangement. I ask—I need—you to be my mate, and One Day Queen.

One Day Queen? Her thoughts were such a whirl, she sought refuge in sarcasm. *Does that mean I'd be the queen one day, or queen for only one d—*

He stopped her thoughts—no easy trick—with a kiss. A long one. A kiss that left her bruised and wanting more and confused and horny and sad and lonesome, all at once.

Artur! Haven't you been listening to a thing I've said? I hate wedding planning! My litany of bitching prompted you to ask me to marry you? How the hell does your mind work, anyway?

I have long wanted to ask you, my Rika. I do not think this comes as a surprise to you.

Well. Not really. He certainly hadn't made any secret of the fact that he wanted to marry her, that he loved her

(like Thomas, he said the same thing and then he left)

and wanted to be with her, always. She had just made the natural assumption that the more he got to know her, the less he would want her. It was perfectly logical.

Artur, I don't know what to say. I mean, I'm really flattered. And pretty much any woman on the planet— tail or legs—would be lucky to get you. I just—I'm not sure I'm the right girl for you. Although, now that she was in her early thirties, "girl" wasn't quite accurate. Except maybe it was, because Artur, who didn't look a day over twenty-five, was actually well into his sixties. Undersea Folk lived long and aged slow.

I beg you to think of it, at least. I do not require your answer this moment, though it would please me as nothing else has. I will wait for you, my Rika, as long as you require.

If you're willing to wait, then I'm willing to give it serious thought, she told him, abruptly squeezing him around the waist. She rested her head against his shoulder and he stroked her short green hair. *Serious thought.*

Then I remain content, he said and kissed her again.

A new start, she thought, kissing him back, and why not? Thomas had Tennian, Jonas had Dr. Barb—where was her chance for happiness? Right in front of her?

Maybe so.

Eleven

Fred popped out onto the deck and walked through her backyard to the pool area, where Jonas was lounging on a patio chair with *Modern Bride* and carefully ignoring her.

She sighed. Jonas in a sulk was about as fun as curdled milk.

She coughed. "Hi."

"Not speaking to you," he said, angrily flipping pages. "As best men go, you suck."

"I know."

"Suck, suck, suck." Each "suck" was punctuated by another turn of the page. "In every possible way, you—Oooh! Now there's a floral arrangement I can live with."

"Jonas—"

"Not speaking to you."

"Listen, I really need to talk to you."

"Listen, I really am not speaking to you. And put some clothes on, wouldya? You've got neighbors."

"Artur asked me to marry him."

Modern Bride went flying in one direction, Jonas's sandal in another as he lunged out of the chair. "What? He did? When?" He clutched his temples and writhed as if on the receiving end of a shock treatment. "Oh, my God! *Two* weddings! I get to plan *a royal frigging wedding*! The guest list! The location! The clothes! And your *mom*! Moon Bimm is going to *freak out*!"

"Jonas—"

"Let's see, it'll have to be somewhere regular people and Undersea Folk can go to, and the food will have to—"

"*Jonas*. I haven't said yes yet," she said, rummaging around in the large plastic chest beneath the porch and extracting a robe. She shrugged into it and plopped down in a poolside chair. "I'm not sure it's the right thing to—"

"*Grab him, you idiot!*"

"You don't have to scream."

Jonas groaned and nearly plummeted into the deep end. "Fred, today's the day. It's finally happened. I'm officially going to kill you. And it's not going to be quick and painless, either, the way I always imagined it. It's going to be long and hideously drawn out, like a bingo tournament."

Fred stifled a yawn. Not even lunchtime, and she was already exhausted. Also, Jonas informed her "today was the day" about every other week.

He was now pacing back and forth in front of her, limping a bit as he was wearing only one sandal. "Let's see, you don't want to marry Artur because . . . um . . . let's see, you don't want to be a princess? And eventually a queen?"

"Actually, no."

"Moron!" he hissed. "Think of all the people you could help! You could change the world, dumb shit! And the jewelry, think of the *jewelry*."

"Because I care so much about the perfect charm bracelet."

"Let's see, what else? You . . . *don't* want the love of a gorgeous hunk who thinks you're beyond swell? Who'll literally treat you like a queen? You *don't* want all the Undersea Folk to *have* to be nice to you, even the ones who have been real assholes? You *don't* want to settle down in time to have kids? You *don't*—"

"You're going supersonic and shrieky. Soon only dogs will hear your litany of abuse."

His teeth came together with a click and she knew, in his mind, he'd just chomped on her nose. "You know what your problem is?"

"I have tons," she admitted.

"Goddamned right! The big one right now is that you're a commitment-phobe."

"Well, yes."

"Don't try to deny it! You— Oh. Okay. Well, admitting you've got a problem is the first step."

"I'm not sure I see myself marrying a merman and living in the Black Sea and being a queen and giving birth to princes and princesses and—I just don't know if that's the life I'm supposed to have."

"Oh, no. You're supposed to die smelly and alone, mourned only by your forty cats."

"I hate cats."

"When you're an old lady (and alone) you'll love 'em. Think *that's* the big plan for your forever after?"

"I don't know the plan," she said patiently. "That's the problem."

"That's not the only problem," Jonas muttered. He stopped in mid-pace and spun to face her. "Waaaaait a minute. This doesn't have anything to do with Priscilla D'Jacqueline, does it?"

"Don't be a dumbass."

"It does! It totally does!"

"And don't call him that."

"Hey, it's not my fault he writes romance novels under a silly-ass pen name."

It was true. Thomas Pearson, M.D., Ph.D., marine biologist and bestselling romance novelist Priscilla D'Jacqueline. He carried Strunk and White's *The Elements of Style*. And a switchblade.

Complicated fellow.

"Artur's proposal and Thomas are separate issues."

"Ha-ha-haaaaaaa."

"It's true," she insisted. "Thomas made his choice. He left . . . more than once, if my math is correct—and you'll recall it's always correct."

"Don't be showing off, *Dr*. Bimm."

"You know I pretty much wrote him off after Tennian got shot and he went all Florence Nightingale on her. They deserve their Happily Ever After."

"I know you *said* you wrote him off. You also say you're a lousy liar, but I'm not so sure about that one. Especially when it comes to your love life. Anybody can lie to themselves."

"Not only am I not in love with Thomas Pearson"— she sighed—"I'm not even sure we're friends. And even if I was in love with him—which I'm not—he's not free to make a commitment. And I'm not sure I'd trust him to stick around if he was. He's really bad at it."

Then, like a genie conjured from a bottle, Thomas Pearson strolled around the side of the house, whistling. He brightened when he saw her and said, "Who's really bad at what?"

"Awesome!" Jonas chortled. "Now it's gonna get good."

Twelve

§

Fred stared at the apparition dressed in a blue oxford shirt with the sleeves rolled up; khaki shorts; loafers without socks (hi, folks, remember the 80s?); diving watch; and no other jewelry (Tennian hasn't dragged him to the altar, or the Undersea Folk equivalent?). Ridiculously tan—but then, Thomas was never one to skulk in a lab. He was an outdoor boy, which she couldn't help respect despite the—

Oh, stop it!

And tall, very tall—he had a good three inches on

her, and she was a healthy six feet—with what most people would call brown hair. She called it russet with gold and red highlights. Never to his face, of course. Hardly ever even to herself, but she had to admit that in his own way, his hair was as interesting as hers . . . and he, at least, didn't have hair of a freakish hue.

The more time he spent in the sun, the lighter it got, and from the way the sun was glinting off his hair, he'd been spending a great deal of time outside indeed.

Sure. Following Tennian's luscious butt hither and yon.

It was longer than usual—he normally kept it short and neat, but now it curled almost to his shoulders, and his golden-brown bangs hung in his face. He flipped them back with a jerk of his head and grinned at her.

Brown eyes—again, not just brown. Brown with (*sigh*) gold flecks. Flecks that twinkled at her whenever he was grinning, just as he was now. Flecks that—oh, Christ, now she sounded like one of his silly-ass romance novels! (Fred was a fan of science journals and true crime stories; *Small Sacrifices* was, in her opinion, one of the finest glimpses into the mind of a sociopath she had ever seen.)

To compensate for the mad feeling that things were still spinning beyond her control, she took refuge behind her temper. "What the hell are you doing here?"

He burst out laughing. "I had a bet with myself—you'd either say, 'What the hell are you doing here?' or, 'How the hell did you find out where I live?' Or possibly, 'Aren't you supposed to be the hell in the Black Sea?' "

"Hey, Thomas." Jonas stuck out a hand, and Thomas crossed the patio in three long strides and shook it. "Long time no, et cetera. Should've guessed since Tennian's around you wouldn't be far behind."

"Oh, she is?" he said vaguely. Then, more briskly, "So what were you two talking about? Looked like life and death from your expressions."

Fred waved a hand, her pulse finally getting back under control after the shock of seeing him. She'd hardly heard what he said . . . only the last comment had really penetrated. "More interviews and crap. Jonas is the wall I wail to."

Jonas leered and looked pleased at the same time, like a man with a bellyache who'd gobbled five antacids.

"Yeah, I saw your picture in *People* last week. You

cut your hair!" He was staring, and smiling, at her chin-length strands.

"All of 'em," she replied. "Also, Jonas is planning his wedding down here."

Thomas rolled his eyes and plopped into a patio chair opposite her. "Oh-oh! That makes you—what? Best— let's see, not best man . . . best woman? Best grump? Best bitch?"

Ignoring Jonas's haw-*haw*, she snapped, "How'd you like to get knocked into the Gulf?"

He propped his tanned legs up on a patio table and stretched his arms behind his head. "Ah, any excuse to have your hands on me."

"I forgot what a big bag of flirt you are."

"But I didn't forget what a cutie *you* are."

"Oh, gawd!" Jonas groaned. "Can't you two just do it and get it over with?"

Thomas laughed long at that one, as if it were the funniest thing he'd ever heard. Fred found it less amusing. Okay, not amusing at all. Okay, the polar opposite of amusing.

"Anyway," Thomas continued, as if she had the teensiest care about what brought him to her rental, "since I can't turn on a television or pick up a newspaper without reading about Undersea Folk or seeing your picture, I thought I'd head down here once I finished my last book. And here you are! Also, this is a small island and everybody knows you're staying here."

"Great," she grumped. "Just what I need."

"Aw, you know you're a Miss Congeniality at heart." He yawned. "So, can I crash here? What does this place have, nine bedrooms?"

"Hardly." Oh, this was too damned much. Stress upon stress upon stress and Thomas fucking Pearson as her new roommate. Not to mention Tennian. Fred could already picture finding long blue strands in her hairbrush. "It's smaller than it looks. On the outside."

"The soul of hospitality, no matter how heavy her duties."

Jonas cleared his throat, which did nothing to alleviate the tension Fred was drowning in. "Hey, check this. I might not be the only one getting married—Artur proposed!"

"To Fred?"

"No, to Dick Cheney. Yeah, to Fred."

Thomas stiffened in, Fred assumed, genuine surprise.

"Artur asked Fred to marry him?" He looked right at her, no twinkle at all in those big brown eyes. "What'd you say?"

"I'm still thinking about it."

He chewed on his lower lip for a moment. "So. I'll just go inside and pick a bedroom, then. My stuff's around the front of the house."

"But I haven't said you could—"

He got up out of the chair and stalked around the corner of the house.

"Well." Jonas coughed again. "And here I thought things might start to settle down a bit." Then, "Dammit! I completely forgot I'm not speaking to you."

"You always do." She sighed and wondered which was the more practical decision: kick Thomas out of her house, hide on the bottom of the pool, or jump into the Gulf and head for Cuba.

Well, shit.

She followed him in.

Thirteen

She had thrown open her (rented) front door and caught Thomas halfway up the steps.

"Look, Pearson, I never said you could—"

"Are you really going to be a princess? And eventually a queen?"

"Actually, the queen's been dead for several years, so—"

"Fred. Cut the shit."

She stared at him and tried to find an answer. Good damn luck. "I'm thinking it over." *Not that it's any of* your *business*. "Jonas reminded me that Artur would treat me, quite literally, like a queen." Not that it's any of your business. "Guys like that are hard to come by."

He smiled sourly.

"Well." She bristled. "They are."

He squinted at her from the sixth stair. "And that's what you want? Royalty? A title? A kingdom?"

"I don't know. I don't know what I want," she admitted. "But Artur and I—we get on, you know. He's shown me things I could never have seen— Shit, I don't have to tell you, I'm sure you've seen plenty of things with Tennian." Besides her tits. "And I won't deny that it's tempting."

Sure. You bet it was tempting. If for no other reason than she wouldn't have to watch Tennian and Thomas slobber all over each other and make li'l hybrids.

"Can't blame you for that one. He's a good man," Thomas said slowly. He had stopped his upward descent and now sat on the stairs, chin cupped in one hand. "It's a good offer. And like you said, he can show you things, and give you things, no one else on the planet can."

"Yes."

"No one would blame you for saying yes, least of all me."

"You've always liked him," she admitted, shutting the door. Jonas, no doubt, would sulk by the pool, giving them the privacy they needed. Or he'd pretend to sulk, which resulted in the same thing.

"Yes. Liked him, admired him, resented him, wanted to beat him, respected him, tormented him, fed him." They both grinned, remembering the trip to Faneuil Hall two years ago when Artur had ordered one of everything—or so it had seemed.

Thomas's smile faded and he sighed, a dreadful sound like dead leaves careening down into a sewer. "You should give it some thought."

Why did he sound so strange? "I am."

"Well." He wouldn't look at her. Why wasn't he looking at her? "That seems pretty sensible."

"Sensible was never my problem."

He smiled. "No."

"Saying 'no' these days seems to be my problem."

He laughed at her.

"I'm serious. I've talked to so many reporters, when I had better things to do, that I've lost count."

"Well. The king will be pleased."

"Yes. How long," she said, "were you planning on staying?

"I dunno," he said vaguely. "Until there's nothing left to see or hear, I s'pose."

"Thanks for being so specific. And Tennian? Will she be shacking up in your room?"

"Tennian is a darling." Fred tried not to flinch. "And will do what she likes; it's her nature. She's an amazing mer—uh, woman."

"Yes." She sought desperately for a change of subject. "I'm guessing your fellowship is done."

"Oh, yeah. Scotland was the last stop—thank God! Did you know I make more money with one book than in two years of being a marine biologist?"

"Great, Priscilla."

"Tennian and I have spent the last few months exploring the planet. She's shown me things." He shook his head and she could see the scientist behind his eyes scheming, scheming. "Things I never dreamed I'd see, not in a hundred lifetimes."

"Well," Fred said stiffly. "How nice for you both."

"And like we've been saying, Artur could do the same."

"Probably."

Thomas sighed. "I'll take the second bedroom on the left."

"That'd be peachy keen."

Oh, sure. Keen. Like an unwanted roommate. Like plague. Like famine.

"I'm not sharing a bathroom with you!" she bawled as he vanished up the steps and down a hallway.

Fourteen

§

A night later, Fred was forced to play hostess. Not that she was having to do any of the actual work, thank God. Jonas had bought the food, Thomas had fired up the grill, and Tennian had shown up with her twin brother and a half dozen fresh lobster.

"Ho, Fredrika Bimm! You recall my brother, Rennan?"

"Vividly." They shook hands gingerly. Rennan wasn't nearly as friendly or open-minded as his sister and was wary of Fred because of her family history. He was a male version of Tennian, with the same blue hair and sapphire-colored eyes. But if he wasn't civil, his sister would kick his ass. She'd done it before. "How'd Tennian drag you here, anyway?"

"It was my honor to come," he replied stiffly.

"Aha! Word's getting out that Artur proposed, I'm guessing. Tsk, tsk, Rennan . . . hedging your bets? How . . . courageous."

He scowled at her, then at his twin when she snickered.

"Well, come on in. Thomas is in the back, trying to fry his eyebrows."

"Fry his—?"

"Hi, Tennian!" Jonas managed not to leer; for a change, Tennian was fully clothed.

Not for the first time, Fred wondered where Undersea Folk got their clothes. The Gap? A mall? An underwater mall? She knew they had gobs of money—every doubloon, antique, gold bar, or what-have-you since man first built ships and lost them to the sea was the property of the king and his people.

"Glad you could make it," Jonas was still yakking, "and—oh, my God, look at the *size* of those things!"

Reasonably sure he meant the lobsters and not Tennian's boobs, Fred relieved her of them and stuffed the wriggling creatures into her fridge. She couldn't eat them, of course (her allergy had been a source of great hilarity to Tennian), but the others would love them.

"I've noticed you don't seem to mind vocalizing so much anymore." This was more scientific curiosity than polite conversation; when they had first met, several months ago, Tennian would hardly say two words out of water, but was quite chatty with her telepathy.

"I practiced with Thomas," the girl replied, inspecting the tablecloth and cloth napkins and dining-room chairs.

I'll bet.

"His Highness regrets," Rennan said, watching his sister with a bemused expression, "he cannot join us for this meal. The good king his father required him to tend to some family business."

"Too bad," Thomas said, sliding open the deck door and popping inside. "He's gonna miss a spread. Hey, Tenn. Hi, Rennan." He embraced Tennian and shook Rennan's forearm, an Undersea Folk–style handshake. "Glad you could make it."

"Oh, I love looking at surface-dweller homes, and I had heard Fredrika was residing in quite a nice one." Tennian flipped a dining-room chair upside down, examined it, and righted it. "And I see I heard correctly!"

"She's so *adorable*," Jonas whispered to Fred. "I'm in love with someone else and I'm still having a hard time resisting her . . . Say, Tennian, could I take a look at your hair?"

Tennian blinked. Fred lied, "Surface dweller custom. We also inspect each other for ticks," so the smaller woman agreed.

Jonas fussed with the woman's long blue strands for a few moments. "Great body. Not too many split ends. What you need is some good conditioner and maybe some gel. I've got both in my rental car."

"Jonas is a scientist, like Fred and me," Thomas explained.

"Ha!" Fred sneered.

"Only he works for a company that makes hair products. He helps think them up."

"I do not wish to put chemicals in my hair," Tennian said soberly. "They would get into the seas. I do not wish to dirty the seas."

"How about a trim, at least?"

"But I don't—"

"I'm taking grill orders," Thomas interrupted. To Jonas: "Give it up." To the group: "So who wants what?"

Tennian and her brother were quite familiar with cooked food, as Undersea Folk frequently held banquets on various deserted islands. They both opted for steak and lobster. Fred decided on a burger and salad. Thomas and Jonas wanted lobster. So Fred found a large pot—hooray for furnished rentals!—and started the water boiling. Thomas disappeared back outside to start grilling.

They sat around the dining-room table, enjoying the sea breeze and gossiping about current events. Unlike his sister, Rennan wasn't keen on being pestered by tourists who wanted to see his tail. If not for his sister's choice, he would have elected to remain hidden from the surface world. The king had given that choice to every one of his subjects, and several thousand of them (Fred had no idea of the exact number) remained off surface-dweller radar . . . literally.

But many, like Tennian, had been curious too long to stay out of sight. And despite being shot by pirates, the smaller woman's enthusiasm for all things surface remained undiminished.

"Water's boiling," Jonas said, peeking into the pot.

"Then drop 'em."

"Chickenshit," he said, not unkindly.

"Can't stand the noise they make," Fred admitted.

"But I thought you couldn't hear us or them outside the water," Rennan said, then *oof*'d as his sister slammed an elbow into his side. "I wasn't being rude," he said, gingerly rubbing his ribs.

"Yes, you *were*; we're not supposed to *tease* her about that. She can't help it if her lady mother is a surface dweller."

"I was only asking," Rennan said, sounding wounded.

"It's okay, Tennian, don't beat him up anymore. I'm not offended."

"Just offensive," Jonas said cheerfully, extracting the wriggling, depressed crustaceans from the fridge.

Fred was momentarily taken aback. No, she had no telepathy on land, couldn't hear a mermaid or a goldfish. But purebreds could. What in the world did a lobster sound like to them as it was being plunged into boiling water? Dear God!

"I meant the *'eeeeeee'* noise when they hit the water. That's what I can't stand."

"That's just the air being shoved out of their shells by the force and heat," Jonas explained for the zillionth time. "They're not actually, y'know, *screaming*. You'd think a marine biologist would know this stuff. Also: gross."

"Well," Tennian began awkwardly, then glanced at her brother, who shrugged. "Well, they do. Ah. Scream. But for less than half a second. They don't like going near the pot, but once they are—ah—inside, they are done."

The dinner party from hell, Fred thought, having no clue what was in store for her in the next half hour. *That's what this is.*

Twenty minutes later, they were all eating with varying degrees of enthusiasm. Tennian and Rennan made short work of their lobsters but took the steaks slower. Thomas was ravenous—he'd been gone all day; Fred had no idea where and was too proud to ask—and wolfed down his meal. Jonas ate methodically and neatly, peppering the twins with questions between bites. And Fred ignored her meat and picked at her salad.

"I met the most charming young surface dweller this

afternoon," Tennian said, slurping the meat out of a lobster leg. She bit off the joint and chewed noisily for a few seconds. "She had perhaps . . . four seasons? Five?"

"Years," Thomas corrected her gently.

"Of course. She had been caught in the riptide and I pulled her back to shore. Poor little one, so frightened! She petted my tail all the way back to shore. Her lady mother was very kind also."

"Well, jeez, I'd hope so," Jonas said, used to Tennian's habit of devouring shellfish, shells and all. "Good for you."

"They all seem very nice," Tennian added. She bit through a lobster claw and extracted the meat, ignoring the melted butter Jonas had placed before her. She squeezed, and the claw shattered and pieces littered her plate. "Other than the ones who shot me, of course."

"Of course," Thomas said, then caught Fred's eye and they snickered together. "Nobody's perfect, though."

"And if anybody'd know, it'd be those two," Jonas teased. "In fact, I—"

There was a sharp rapping at the front door. Fred groaned inwardly and got up. "Maybe Artur could make it after all."

The twins shook their heads in unison. "He would have told us on his way."

"God, I'd *love* to be telepathic," Jonas was saying as Fred made her way to the door. "Way more efficient than flapping my gums all day long."

"Yes," the twins said in unison.

Another hard rap, and Fred pulled the door open. "All right, no need to knock it down." She stared at the man. "Who the hell are you?"

He was almost exactly her height—perhaps an inch taller. His hair was the exact color of hers, only it was shoulder-length. His eyes were also a vivid green, the color of the ocean in high summer. His face was smooth and unlined; he looked like he was in his mid-twenties.

Fred wasn't fooled; with that coloring he had to be Undersea Folk. And they aged beautifully. He could have been in his fifties, or barely drinking age.

He was wearing jeans, tennis shoes, and a red polo shirt. His fingers were long and, as he stretched out his hand for her to shake, strong. He was lightly tanned, and really pretty good-looking.

"Crashing the party?" She managed to extract her hand before he broke any bones.

"Yes, several years too late, Fredrika. Do you not recognize me?"

"Should I?"

"Has your lady mother never described me?"

Fred blinked.

The hair.

The eyes.

Oh man oh man ohmanohmanohman.

Her insides seemed to lock up and then slither to the bottom of her stomach. She felt her left eye twitch in a stress spasm. Oh, this was perfect. Icing on the wedding cake, so to speak. Christ.

"Don't even tell me."

"I'm—"

"I said don't tell me!"

"—your father. My name is Farrem."

From behind, a baritone yowl from Rennan: "Traitor!"

And also from behind, Tennian: "Get away from her right now, you filth!"

A chair fell over and she could hear rapidly approaching footsteps. Tennian, with the height of a pygmy and the courage of a rabid ape, launching herself, no doubt.

Fred turned, braced herself, and caught the woman by the elbows—barely. They both toppled backward, into Fred's father, and out the door onto the sidewalk.

Fifteen

For a few minutes Fred felt like a character in a Bugs Bunny cartoon—everything was whirling fists and rolling around on the lawn and kicking feet. All that was missing was the cloud of dust and the darting stars.

Finally, *finally* she was able to get to her feet and between her (groan) father and Tennian, making the time-out sign from football and instantly realizing neither of them probably knew what it meant.

"Cut it *out*!" she shrieked, booting Tennian in the

ankle and hooking an elbow into her father's gut. It was like elbowing plywood.

Tennian lunged and Fred backed up fast, forcing her father to back up as well. "You remove yourself from the lady's property this moment or I shall—"

Fred was shoved forward as her father first planted his feet and then started forward. It occurred to her that both of them had at least twice her strength. "I have a perfect right to see my daughter on land, you pious—"

"I mean it, you guys. Not here, not on my front lawn; I'm getting dizzy and my damned dinner's getting cold!"

"But he is a most foul—"

"I did not wish for this and I—"

"*Cut it out!*"

Sulky silence. Not to mention staring eyes . . . everyone else had piled out the front door to watch the fight. Jonas and Thomas seemed fascinated. Rennan looked horrified and amused at the same time; it was well known that his twin was the hard-ass.

Fred sighed. Pushed her hair out of her eyes. Glared at them both. "You guys better come inside."

"I am grateful for your hos—"

"But, Fredrika! He is a most loathsome—"

"Tennian, he's coming in. You can come in, too, or stay out here on the lawn. Or go jump in the ocean. But he's coming in."

"So . . . he's coming in?" Jonas was grinning, looking from father to daughter to father. "Hey there, Fred's Dad. Nice to meetcha. You want a burger, a lobster, or a steak?"

Sixteen

🐚

Rennan and Tennian wouldn't stay.

"Oh, come on," Jonas, ever the peacemaker, coaxed. "Look how much lobster's left! Without you chewing on the things, all that shell is going to go to waste."

"We cannot remain under the roof with a traitor to the royal blood," Tennian said stiffly, and Fred remembered that Artur was her cousin. She, probably more than the average Undersea Folk, took Fred's father's betrayal more personally than most. "I do not mean to give offense, Fredrika."

"Farewell," her twin added, holding the door for his sister. "The food was very fine."

"Run along, children," her father said. Fred had to admit, he seemed pretty unruffled at the snub. Almost . . . amused?

She sort of liked him for it.

The twins stomped out looking (Fred had to admit it) exactly like kids throwing a tantrum.

"So!" Farrem said brightly, sitting down in Tennian's chair. "Are you going to eat that lobster?"

Seventeen

"This is a little awkward—" Fred began, only to be interrupted by Jonas.

"No, it's cool! It's so cool that you showed up now! My God . . . so . . . many . . . questions . . ." Jonas clutched his temples. "Let's start with the big one. Does inherent grumpiness run in your side of the family? Because she sure didn't get it from her mom. And do you take pleasure in looking as unattractive as you can at every opp—"

Farrem laughed, an easy, deep sound. "I will gladly

answer your questions, good sir, but perhaps introductions could come first?"

"If you're expecting your one and only daughter to remember protocol, you're gonna have a long damn wait," Thomas said, smiling a little. Fred wasn't fooled. Thomas might look and sound casual, as if this were any other get-together, but she knew the scientist in him wanted to stick Farrem in a lab and run several hundred tests. And right now!

"Am I?" Fred asked.

"Are you what, my own?" Farrem bit off a lobster claw and crunched contentedly.

"Your one and only daughter."

Farrem laughed. "As far as I know! Certainly you're the most famous of my offspring, even if I had several dozen to keep track of. I saw you on the television box and thought, could that be the product of that delightful night on a Cape Cod beach? You must admit . . ." *Crunch. Crunch.* ". . . we look a great deal alike."

"Yeah, I was noticing that, too." One thing about Undersea Folk . . . the only ones who shared the same coloring were blood relatives, like Artur and the king, or Tennian and her brother. "Well, you asked about intros. This is my best friend, Jonas, and this is my colleague—"

"Colleague?" Thomas cried with mock hurt. "Is that all we are to each other, you heartless harpy?"

"—Dr. Thomas Pearson. Guys, this is—well— Farrem." She wasn't ready to call him "Dad." Shit, her stepfather, Sam, had raised her (he'd married her mother, Moon, while she was knocked up with Fred) and she didn't even call *him* Dad. "My, uh, biological father."

"It pleases me to meet such gentlemen over my daughter's table." *Crunch.* "Fredrika, tell me—how is your lady mother?"

"Hot," Jonas said.

Fred glared. Jonas's crush on her mother got more disturbing every year. When they were nine it wasn't too creepy, but now . . . "Moon's fine." *In fact, I'm going to have to make a phone call. Right now.* "She thinks you're dead."

Farrem's smile dropped away like someone had snatched it. "To many of our folk, I am. Or as good as."

"So why are you here now?" Thomas asked.

"Is it not obvious, Dr. Pearson? The king could banish me from his kingdom . . . but not from the surface. I confess I could scarce believe my eyes when I started seeing the news reports."

"You and most of the rest of the planet."

"Indeed! And now that my folk have begun making themselves known to surface dwellers . . ." Farrem shrugged and crunched into a claw. "It seemed an opportune time to reemerge."

"I'm sure the others will be thrilled," Fred said dryly, remembering the reaction of the twins.

"That," Farrem said coolly, "is their problem and not mine. Besides, how could I stay away when every time I turned on the television box my own eyes were staring out at me?"

Fred could feel herself start to blush, and fought it. Still. A nice thing for him to say. Gracious, even, because she was no beauty, and *he* was really handsome.

"I must admit, I was astonished—not only to see you, but to see my own people coming out of the sea. Astonishing. Truly." He shook his head. "After centuries of hiding . . ."

"But what's your plan? I mean, Fred says you got

kicked out—banished or whatever—after, uh . . . So what's your plan?"

"I was intemperate and willful in my youth," Farrem said evenly, "and reached too high. I was deservedly slapped down and have been paying the price for over three decades. I earned my banishment. But the king cannot keep me from the surface, and now that my people are out *here* . . ." He shrugged. "My plan is atonement. I wish to show the royal family I am no threat . . . Not that, after defeating me, they need such assurances! And eventually . . . maybe . . . acceptance."

Fred thought about the twins and didn't think dear old Dad should hold his breath on that one.

"It will take time," he said, practically reading her mind. "But then, if you know our people, Fredrika, you know that time, at least, is something most of us have much of. Comparatively speaking," he added with an apologetic glance at Thomas and Jonas.

"You should stay here while you put Operation Atonement into action," Jonas said. "Fred has tons of room."

Fred, who had raised the can of Coke to her mouth, nearly crushed it. "What?" Oh, this was too much!

"Of course, I would never impose," her father said hastily, which made Fred feel bad, which made her mad.

Which made her *furious* at Jonas. Tons of room, her scaled ass! If her math was correct, there was exactly one empty bedroom left . . . which she was about to offer to her long-lost father. She knew, knew, *knew* renting a four-bedroom house was an exercise in madness.

On the upside, with no more bedrooms to offer, that'd be the end of drop-in guests. Probably. Maybe.

"It's no imposition," she lied, wishing she dared toss Jonas into the pool. "We can—uh—" What did fathers and daughters *do*, exactly? Go to father/daughter picnics? Was he going to teach her to drive? Would she share her dating debacles with him? God, he wouldn't think he had to tell her about the birds and the bees, would he? "Upstairs, last door on the left."

"Then if you will excuse me, I will get settled." He stood so quickly they hardly saw him move, and bowed to them. "My thanks for the welcome, the meal, the conversation, and the very fine hospitality."

They watched him climb the stairs, and then Thomas leaned in and murmured, "Your old man's got style to spare."

"I wonder if he was so polite when he tried to kill the king."

"C'mon, Fred." Jonas snatched her Coke and took a healthy guzzle. "He said it himself—he was a jerk when he was young. Seems to run in the family."

"How'd you like to hit the pool? From the second story? Through a closed window?"

He ignored her threats, as he had for decades. "It was thirty years ago. He's sorry now, I bet. But that's not even the important thing."

"Oh, do tell, Jonas." She grabbed her Coke back. "What's the important thing?"

"Deciding whether or not to call Moon."

Her mother! Ack. Jonas was right, curse his eyes. She cringed, picturing the call.

And then the visit.

Better get it over with.

Eighteen

"Now!" Moon Bimm said briskly. She and her husband, Sam, had taken a cab from the airport and had only now arrived at Fred's house. "What's this all about, Fred? Why so mysterious on the phone? If you're trying to get out of helping Jonas plan his wedding, you can just stop it right now."

"But how'd you even know Jonas—"

"He called me."

"What?"

Moon blinked. "He calls almost every week."

"Oh, for the love of—"

"Do you have any herbal tea?"

"No, I have beer and soda."

"Fred, how can you treat your body so badly? It is a sacred temple, a gift—particularly yours! Vitamin water and salads, that's how you could best show your body how grateful you are for the gift of such a hallowed vessel."

Fred ground her teeth. Moon had never quite let go of the hippie thing, and it was maddening. Also, she was a *rich* hippie, like that wasn't a weird-ass paradox. Sam came from tons of money.

And, though she wasn't about to admit it to Jonas, her mother was in damned fine shape for a woman in her fifties. A short, good-looking blonde with silver streaks running through her shoulder-length hair, Moon was plump where women are supposed to be plump, with laugh lines and a near-permanent smile. She didn't dress like the wife of a millionaire, preferring faded T-shirts and jeans.

Sam, Fred's stepfather, was as mild-mannered as Fred was not. Tall, balding, with a gray-streaked ponytail, he, also, didn't dress like a millionaire. More like a struggling artist.

Although she could never tell him so, she loved him and honored him for not fleeing when he realized his new wife had popped out a mermaid. He had even, memorably, tried to teach her how to swim.

It had gone badly. He'd had to be rescued from the YMCA pool. But that wasn't the point.

"Mom, I didn't call you guys down here so you could lecture me about my Coke habit. The thing is—"

"Are you nervous about *60 Minutes*? Because you'll be fine," Sam said, opening the fridge and peering inside. "You've been doing fine in all your interviews."

"Thank goodness for TiVo," Moon added. "Otherwise we couldn't keep up with all your appearances."

"Your mother is keeping a scrapbook," Sam said, popping a beer. He, unlike Moon, didn't mind polluting his sacred temple with the occasional can of Bud.

"Don't even tell me."

"It's getting huge."

"Sam, seriously! Don't tell me. Listen. Mom. And, uh, Sam. Now don't freak out."

"Oh, my God!" Moon darted forward and seized

Fred's cold hands (they were always cold) in her warm ones. "You're pregnant!"

Fred, a full head taller than her petite, sweetly plump mother, blanched and tried to pull away. Weirdly, it was difficult—Moon had quite a grip when she wanted. "Mom, I'm not— Jeez, ease up, will you? My fingers are going numb. I'm not pregnant. You have to have sex to get pregnant and I'm in the middle of a three-year dry spell."

"Oh, now that's just ridiculous! Prince Artur would have sex with you in half a second, and I'll bet that nice Dr. Pearson would, t—"

"Mom, we are not. Discussing. My arid. Sex life."

"But it's not wrong to share what God has given you with a man you—"

"Mom!" Fred nearly howled.

"Try not to scream, hon," Sam said, sipping contentedly at his Bud. "It's not even noon."

Fred extracted herself from her mother's grip with no small difficulty, took a swig of Sam's beer, then sucked in a breath and tried again.

"Thanks for coming so fast. I've got some news and I wanted to tell you in person."

"Well," Sam said reasonably, "don't keep us in suspense."

The front door opened and Jonas called, "Hey, new rental car in the driveway—is your hot mom here?"

Fred moaned. Sam grinned, got up, pulled out another beer, and handed it to her. Moon turned to greet Fred's unbelievably irritating friend.

"Jonas, you bad boy, like I don't know you're in love with a perfectly beautiful woman."

"Ah, Moon." He hugged her mother so hard, the woman's feet left the floor. "You never forget your first crush. So, what d'you think of the news?"

"We were just—"

"*I* think she should say yes. Don't you want to have a princess in the family?"

Fred finished her beer in four gulps.

"*What?* You mean Prince Artur finally asked you to marry him?"

"Mom . . ."

"But that's wonderful! You can settle down and have children and help the Undersea Folk and—and—"

Shocking everyone in the room, Moon burst into tears.

Nineteen

🌊

Pandemonium. Shouts. Threats. Tears. Kleenex. More shouts. More tears.

"Mom, what *is* it?"

"I'm so sorry," she sobbed. "I'm happy for you, I swear I am."

"I can tell," Fred replied, moderately horrified.

"Only . . . you'll have to go live with him. In the castle under the Black Sea. And I'll never see you. Not like I do now. How can I?"

"But I hardly ever visit unless—"

"I can't even visit . . . Dr. Pearson told me the pressure alone would kill a surface dweller; that's why they built their home base there. This—" She waved a hand, vaguely indicating Sanibel Island. "This isn't real. It's a fake castle; the king's playing it safe, you explained it to me. And I understand. I truly do."

"You don't look like you understand," Fred said doubtfully.

"But if you got married—if you were a member of the royal family—you'd have to move. To the other side of the planet. *Beneath* the other side of the planet. And I don't want—you're my only—"

"Mom, for God's sake." Fred could count on one hand how many times she'd seen her mother cry. It was frightening and frustrating and weird, all at once. "That's not even my news, thank you very much, *Jonas*."

"Well, how was I supposed to know you wouldn't mention, oh, I dunno, *a royal marriage proposal* to your mom?"

Moon sniffed and blinked up at her daughter. "You mean he didn't propose?"

"Oh, he proposed. I just haven't made up my mind."

Moon looked horrified even as Jonas was busily

blotting her cheeks with Kleenex. "But then I've messed it up! You'll factor my reaction into your decision-making!"

"When has she ever, Moon?" Sam asked mildly, which was just the right thing to say. Everyone calmed down.

She sniffled again. "But then what *is* your news?"

"Well. It's like this. My father—my biological, Undersea Folk father—is alive."

Moon and Sam stared at her.

"Blow," Jonas ordered, and Moon blew into the Kleenex.

"And staying here. With me."

More staring.

"And he was hoping to see you again. If your—uh—" She turned to Jonas. "How'd he put it?"

" 'If he who is her mate in no way objects,' " Jonas parroted. "Guy talks like a book. A good book," he added hastily, "but still. A book. I mean, I've got a degree in chemical engineering and *I* don't talk like a book."

"More like a comic. Anyway, 'he who is her mate' . . .

that'd be you," she told Sam. "He'd like to see her again if you don't mind."

"I don't mind," Sam said. "I'd like to meet him myself."

"Awww. Just like a family reunion," Jonas said. "Actually, it *is* a family reunion. Here," he added, handing Moon more Kleenex. "Keep the box."

Twenty

Before things could settle down, the front door opened and Farrem walked in. Limped in, actually, and he had the beginning of a gorgeous black eye.

Fred was on her feet before she knew she was going to stand. "Jesus Christ! What happened to you?"

"Ran into three or four of the old guard," he said with dry good humor. "They reminded me that the rash actions of my youth have not been forgotten." He touched his swelling eye and grinned, showing the exceedingly sharp teeth common to Undersea Folk. Sam nearly choked on his beer—Fred had inherited her mother's teeth. "Forcefully. But who is this? Not Fred's lady mother and he who is her mate?"

"H-hello," Moon said, wiping her face. Then she got a closer look as Farrem closed the distance between them and gasped. "My God! You haven't aged a day!"

He laughed and took her small hands in his. "If only that were true, Madame Bimm."

"Please." She smiled wryly. "I think you can call me Moon."

"With your mate's kind permission," Farrem said, bowing slightly in Sam's direction. Sam looked nonplussed for a moment, then nodded back.

Moon cleared her throat. "Are you—are you in trouble? Because you've come back?"

"Of course," he replied easily. "Deservedly so. I hope to win my people over in another decade or so."

Fred was struck, once again, at how Undersea Folk thought nothing of a task that might take twenty or thirty years. By comparison, surface dwellers were fruit flies running around trying to accomplish everything in a nine-day life span.

Did I just refer to my mother's people as flies?

Eesh.

"—enough of my nonsense. What have you been doing these past decades?"

"Well, raising your daughter, of course." Moon laughed. "Though once she was about thirteen or so she stopped listening to me."

"Yes, that is typical among our kind."

"Our kind, too," Sam said, smiling a little.

"And it is on just this basis that King Mekkam decided to let his people reveal themselves, I suspect. In many ways, we are not so different."

"If you say so, pal," Jonas said, sounding fairly unconvinced. Fred jumped; he'd been so uncharacteristically quiet she'd forgotten he was there. "I guess anyone can get past the tail. And the teeth. And the breathing underwater thing. And the—"

"Don't you have a wedding to plan?"

"As a matter of fact," Jonas said with stiff dignity, "I'm late for a tux fitting right this minute."

"So run along."

"I will. See you guys later." And right before he went out the door he said, "Also my fiancée will be here tonight and I don't want to hear any bitching about it, good-bye!"

"Wait!" Fred yelled, and the door slammed.

She cursed vividly enough to make Farrem raise his eyebrows.

Twenty-one

"Well, that's just great." Fred fumed. "I knew I should have just gotten a room at the Super 8."

"You remind me of my mother," Farrem commented. "She often complained about events that did not truly upset her."

"You stay out of this. Dr. Barb. Great! Well, I guess I can try to quit again."

"Pardon, what?"

"Never mind, Farrem."

"She keeps trying to quit her job in Boston, and her boss keeps not letting her," Moon offered.

"Never *mind*. Suffice it to say I lead a stupidly complicated life."

The front door slammed open hard enough to shake part of the house, and a furious Prince Artur stood in the doorway.

"Case in point." Fred sighed as the prince stomped toward them. "You know, surface dwellers do this thing called knocking. If you're going to hang out on top of the planet as opposed to beneath the waves, you might want to—"

"So it is true," Artur hissed, eyeing Farrem the way you'd look at a cockroach in your cereal bowl. "I would never have believed it to be had I not seen it myself."

Farrem turned slowly. "My prince," he said calmly.

"You will remove yourself from the home of she-who-will-be-my-mate at once."

"How can he?" Fred asked. "He's staying in one of the guest rooms upstairs. His stuff's probably all over the bathroom."

Artur actually clutched his head. "I had heard that as well, but put it down to uninformed rumor."

"And that's quite enough of telling my houseguests what to do. That's *my* job."

"Fredrika, I insist this man leave your home at once."

"*This man* is my father, so tough nuts."

"I do not wish to be the cause of strife between you and the prince," Farrem said. "I shall go."

"Sit your ass back down," Fred ordered. Farrem arched his eyebrows but obeyed.

Then she turned to Artur. "And you! Don't come barging into my house without knocking and then start ordering people around. In case you haven't noticed, *Prince*, this isn't your domain. It's mine!"

Sam cleared his throat. "Technically, that's not—"

"You want to boss people around in the Mariana Trench, fine. Don't pull that shit in my house."

Artur blinked, scowled, and blinked harder. Farrem brought a hand up to cover his mouth; his eyes were wide and Fred suspected he was hiding a smile.

"Rika, this man is—"

"My father. Whom I've never met. Whom I'm getting to know. Who is a guest in my house."

"I think you might like him," Moon piped up, "if you gave him a chance, Artur."

"He tried to kill my father, good lady."

"Oh. Well, that's harder to forgive," Moon admitted. "But he said himself, he was just a kid when——"

"——he committed treason."

"I will go," Farrem said.

"Freeze," Fred ordered. Thinking, *Why am I fighting so hard for this? Because it's going to stick in Artur's craw? So my mom can get to know my dad? So I can? Why?* "I suppose Tennian practically broke a leg getting to you to blab."

"Tennian did her duty."

"Yeah, she's not biased or anything."

"Fredrika," Farrem said quietly. "The royal family has every reason to distrust my motivations."

"I get it, I get it. Listen, Artur, it was thirty years ago, okay? He was just a kid. Your dad banished him. *Banished* him. For three decades he hasn't seen another member of his own species. Doesn't that count for anything?"

Scowling silence.

"Besides, all this high-handed stuff is no way to get

me to agree to marry you," she teased, hoping he'd lighten up.

Farrem's green eyes opened wide. "*Marry?* By the king, of course!" He literally slapped himself on the forehead. "When you came in, you called her she-who— but I admit I was much more occupied watching your hands than listening—so you'll be my princess, and one day my queen?" He shook his head so hard, green strands flew. "Astonishing! O irony, how she makes slaves of us all!"

"That's beautiful, Farrem," Moon breathed.

"I haven't said yes yet, so calm down. And you!" She turned back to Artur, who was looking sulky as well as annoyed. "I can read you like a book, Artur. You're thinking now that my dad has turned up alive and well, even *more* of the Undersea Folk won't like me. It was one thing when everyone assumed he was dead. But him showing up . . . it might make marrying me a bit trickier, especially if the court of public opinion doesn't come back in your favor."

"I would hope," he replied stiffly, "I am not as shallow as that."

"Well, Artur, so would I."

"Fred!" Moon gasped.

She turned. "Don't you think you and Sam should—"

And then, for the dozenth time (at least), her front door opened and Thomas was racing into the room. "Fred, Artur found out your father's in town and he's coming over here to—oh." He screeched to a halt, narrowly avoiding slamming into the table. "You, uh, already know."

Fred was resting her forehead on the table. "I want all my keys back," she said into the wood.

Twenty-two

🦐

An hour later, her parents had departed for their hotel, Artur had dived off the dock in a sulk, Farrem had retired upstairs, and Fred and Thomas were drinking the last of the beer.

"What a day," she moaned. "And it's barely half over!"

Thomas grinned at her. "A week with you is more exciting than a year anywhere else."

"Cut the shit," she said morosely. "I'm in no mood for idle flattery."

"Who said it was idle?"

"Idle is your middle name. I s'pose Tennian blabbed that Artur was coming."

"Tennian?" Thomas looked puzzled. "I haven't seen her since dinner last night."

"What are you talking about? Aren't you staying with her? Or she with you? Or however you guys worked out the details? Are you shacked up in the URV, or what?"

"What are you talking about?"

"You know what? Never mind, I don't want to know."

Thomas was looking more and more mystified. "Fred, what the hell are you babbling about? Tennian and I are just friends."

"I don't babble, and what the hell are *you* babbling about? You guys sailed off together last fall to live happily ever after."

Thomas laughed at her. "The hell we did! I mean, we went off together, but I went with her first strictly as her doctor—she *was* shot, you'll recall."

"Well, she *did* board a pirate ship."

"True," he admitted.

"And you two were making goo-goo eyes at each other."

"No, we weren't."

"I was there!"

"I'm really fond of her, okay? I thought—think—she's a fascinating individual. But I was never in love with her."

Fred tried to digest this, but he wouldn't stop talking, so it was a lot to take in.

"And don't forget about the new book I've been working on."

"*Love in the Time of Fish?*"

"*The Anatomy and Physiology of* Homo Nautilus."

"Oh," Fred said. "That." Luckily, this time she managed not to go off into gales of humiliating laughter when he told her.

And he was *still talking.* "So far as I know, I'm the only doctor on the planet who's treated surface dwellers *and* Undersea Folk. You should do it, too, Fred."

She was having major trouble tracking the conversation. "What?"

"Write a book. You could write your life story—or at least, a book about the Undersea Folk. Or best of all, a book about the Undersea Folk through the eyes of the only hybrid on the planet. It'd sell in about two seconds. You'd be a bestselling author!"

"I've got enough fame, thanks. But about you and Tennian—"

"Well, like I said, Tennian's been a big help with my book. And to pay me back for taking care of her, she showed me some unbelievable things."

"I'll bet."

He ignored the jibe. "I mean, just knowing you, I thought I'd seen things, but she—" He shook his head. "You know, you really need to get over to the Black Sea and see all the underwater castles. Thanks to the URV, the pressure didn't squash me like a caterpillar."

The URV—Underwater RV—was the submarine Thomas had had built eighteen months ago . . . it had allowed him to observe various Undersea Folk gatherings. It was also ridiculously comfortable, tricked out with a kitchen and a bedroom, among other things.

"So you broke up?" Fred said through numb lips.

"What, broke up? We were never dating."

Fred did her famous impersonation of a goldfish; her mouth popped open, then closed, then popped open again. Her thoughts, chaotic enough this week, were whirling.

Stop the roller coaster, I want to get off!

Why hadn't he—why had she assumed—what did this mean for her relationship with Artur—why hadn't she known this before Artur proposed—why had she so stupidly jumped to conclusions—why—why—why—?

"Are you all right?" Thomas asked, polishing off the last beer. "You look a little green. Even for you."

"It's just—it's just that kind of week," she managed, thinking, *He must never, never know what I assumed, or what I hoped, or the effect his little announcement had on me. Never.*

If he really loved her, he wouldn't keep going off on months-long trips. If he really loved her, he would have stayed in touch while he was in Scotland, the Black Sea, wherever.

And that was fine . . . he had never promised her a damned thing.

But it was clear to her now what her answer to Artur must be.

Twenty-three

Later that night, Fred sat quietly on the couch, pretending to read about herself in *Time*. Around her, the bustle of an impromptu dinner party went on. And on.

Her mother and Sam had come back with groceries, and once again Thomas was manning the grill. Jonas had returned with a catalogue of tuxes, the one he'd chosen clearly marked. Black tuxedo, red cummerbund, yak-yak-yak. He'd also informed her she would be trying on bridesmaid dresses the next day at ten.

And the hell marches on . . .

Dr. Barb, Jonas's fiancée and Barb's (former?) boss at the New England Aquarium, was also at the house. She had arrived promptly at four, refused both a written and verbal resignation, then pretended she wasn't dying for Fred to shift to her tail.

Fred had given in, diving into the deep end of the pool and shifting to tail form more or less without thought. There was a method to her madness; she'd tried to resign yet again while Dr. Barb was fairly dazzled, and it hadn't worked. Yet again.

"Dr. Bimm, if I may—" Dr. Barb was always perfectly polite, even squatting beside a pool dressed in madras shorts and a white button-down, talking to a mermaid. "How do you breathe underwater? Do you have internal gills? And if so, do they—"

"No. I just pull oxygen from the water through my cells. I hold my breath, of course, but I still get plenty of air, so to speak."

"But you don't know for sure?"

"Well, I've never seen a post on a fellow Undersea Folk, so I couldn't say for sure . . ."

"But, Dr. Bimm, you're a marine biologist."

"Really? I forgot all about that. So that's what that diploma is for . . ."

"Surely you're curious about your own . . . ah . . . unique physiology. Blood tests at the very least could . . ."

"I didn't want to call attention to myself in college. Or grad school. Or anywhere," she said shortly, and that was the end of that. At least, Dr. Barb was too polite to bug her further.

But Fred knew the real reason she, an alleged scientist, knew so little about her own body: she had been a freak all her life. She had no interest in running tests that confirmed her freakishness. She wanted to blend, not call attention to herself. (How annoying to find that hair dye never took; it washed out the moment she grew her tail . . . thus, cursed with green freak hair.) Ignorance, at least in this one case, was bliss.

Well. Cowardice, really. But dammit, she was fine with that. She'd had a loaded gun in her face, for Christ's sake. She'd been *shot*, even. She was entitled to be a coward in the minor area of her extreme freakish appearance.

Now, Dr. Barb and Jonas were snuggling at the

dining-room table and tossing the salad. Or snuggling the salad and tossing each other; Fred was careful not to look too closely. The scenes she'd walked in on starring the two of them . . . *yurrgh*.

And now what the hell was this? There was a funny sound reverberating through the house. Fred looked up from reading about herself

("That's the dumbest question you've asked so far.")

and listened, puzzled. It sounded both familiar and strange at the same time. She'd heard that sound before in her life, but under which circumstances? So hauntingly familiar . . . it was on the tip of her tongue . . . it was . . . was . . .

The doorbell!

No wonder she couldn't place the sound, she thought as she got up to answer it. Nobody ever used it! Most of them didn't even knock.

"Someone's at the door!" Jonas yelled, showing Moon a picture of his tux.

"I've got it," she called back. She opened it and saw Tennian standing with another Undersea Folk. This new mermaid had such striking coloring, she made Tennian seem almost drab: waist-length, deep purple hair, and

eyes the color of wet violets. Pale skin, almost milky—
the complexion of an Irish milkmaid, with the faintest
blush at her cheeks. She came up to Fred's shoulder and
was, without question, the most beautiful woman Fred
had ever seen.

"Whoa," she managed before she could stop herself.

"Good evening, Fredrika Bimm. This is my friend
Wennd."

Wennd said nothing, merely bowed her head in
greeting.

"Well, hi. What brings you two here?"

Wennd shot an anxious glance at Tennian, who said,
"Wennd is really very curious about surface dwellers.
But word of what happened to me has spread and she's
somewhat . . . apprehensive. I was hoping you would
perhaps introduce her to your friends and family, who
are really very nice surface dwellers and won't shoot
anyone."

"Probably," Fred said. "You sure, Wennd? Haven't
you heard? I come from a short, undistinguished line of
traitors."

Wennd's gorgeous purple eyes widened. "That was
your sire. Not you."

Fred knew, then, that Wennd was young. So damned hard to tell with these guys; she could have been twenty or fifty. She'd noticed the real grudge holders were the ones who had been around during her father's disastrous attempt at a coup. But the younger generation . . . the ones who hadn't had to fight, hadn't had to choose sides . . .

"Sure," she said, stepping back. "Come on in. This place is crawling with unwanted g—uh, surface dwellers."

Twenty-four

Fred led the two women into the main dining area. "Guys? Guys! Jonas, put that catalogue away before I make you eat it. Thomas, the grill can wait for ten seconds. Sam, we're out of beer so stop looking."

"But you should take another look at the tux so when you try on—"

"But the temp on the grill is just right, I need to put the burgers—"

"How can you possibly be out of beer?"

"*Guys.* Most of you already know Tennian. This is

her friend Wennd. She thinks surface dwellers are dangerous sociopaths and I admit, I couldn't think of much to say in our defense."

"I didn't say that exactly," Wennd almost whispered. Even her voice was beautiful, tinkly and sweet. Fred was ready to smack her. It was positively sickening when one person got every single fabulous attribute available. Probably a tomcat in the sack, too. "It's quite nice to meet you all."

Jonas and Thomas managed to close their mouths long enough to shake her forearm, the traditional greeting for Undersea Folk. Moon gently bullied her into having a seat at the table, and Sam offered her a large glass of water . . . the beverage of choice for most Undersea Folk, who got terribly thirsty after being out of the water for any length of time.

Out of all the men, he was the only one not staring at the beauty. This surprised Fred not at all. Sam had never, ever looked at another woman since he'd hooked up with Moon. It was touching, yet creepy.

"So where are you from, Wennd, dear?" Moon asked.

"I live in the Indian Ocean, mostly," Wennd whispered.

"Oh! That's . . . er . . ."

"Third largest ocean in the world, Mom," Fred said. "North border, Asia."

"West border," Thomas piped up, not to be out-flanked, "Africa, bordered on the east by Indochina, the Sunda—"

"—Islands and Australia," Fred finished tri-umphantly. "How about *that*?"

"Wow," Jonas said. "It's the Battle o' the Geeks. I think I nodded off around Indochina."

"But I already know those things," Wennd practically whispered. Fred felt like giving her a megaphone.

"She was enlightening *me*, dear." Moon laughed. "Geography was never my strong point."

"So what brings you here?" Jonas asked.

Wennd looked around cautiously, then replied, "As you all seem to have the ear of the king or the prince, I will guess it is all right to confide. I was one of the citizens the king asked to come here."

"Right!" Thomas snapped his fingers. "To preserve the illusion that your headquarters are here, not the Black Sea."

"Yes, Dr. Pearson, that is correct."

"How'd you know my—"

"Tennian described all of you."

"No doubt," Fred muttered. A thought struck her: "The illusion is working great. You know, other than Artur and King Mekkam, I don't think I've met anyone who lives in the Black Sea, where the real castles are."

"Well, who's fault is that, Miss I Haven't Made Up My Mind?" Jonas said. "You marry Artur and you'll probably be there in forty-eight hours."

"Doubtful," Fred said. "I can't swim as fast as he can."

"Yeah, but *you* have frequent flyer miles."

Fred snickered. *Good one.*

"You will join us for dinner," Moon said, pretending it was a question. Wennd must have had a mom much like Moon, because she didn't even try to demur.

"Hello," Dr. Barb said. She'd been gaping at the violet-haired mermaid during the entire discussion. "I'm Dr. Barbara Robinson. I run the New England Aquarium. May I ask a personal question about your species?"

"Yes."

"Does your coloring run in your family? Or is it natural to, say, a country of Undersea Folk?"

Wennd's big eyes widened. "Do you mean, does my mother have purple hair, or does everyone who lives in the Indian Ocean have purple hair?"

"Yes, it's a matter of—"

But Dr. Barb had to quit, because Wennd had burst into a loud, honking laugh. It was such a contrast to her shy demeanor and whispery voice, half the room flinched. She sounded like a Canadian goose chasing away a predator.

"So . . . no?" Sam asked.

Wennd was actually clutching her stomach and honking away.

"Wennd," Tennian said reproachfully. "Please don't laugh at my friends."

"Why not?" Fred asked. "I do it all the time."

"I beg your pardon," Wennd gasped. "I am so sorry. Truly. I just—does everyone in the American state of Florida have yellow hair and blue eyes? Because they are in proximity with each other?"

"Point," Jonas admitted. "Or assuming that if your mom is a redhead, everyone she's related to would be, too." Pause. Blond Jonas added, "*My* mom's a red-head."

Thomas was spinning the spatula in his grip like it was a six-shooter. "Hamburger or hot dog?"

"Just more water, if you please." When Moon opened her mouth to bully Wennd into eating, the mermaid added, "Tennian and I ran into a bull shark on the way here. I'm really not hungry at all."

"You two took on a *bull*? By yourselves?" Thomas looked horrified and Fred couldn't blame the ignorant sap. He still didn't comprehend how strong, fast, and predatory full-blooded Undersea Folk were. "Tell me it was a baby. Or an immature female. Or—"

"It was a male, about—what? Six feet? Two hundred pounds?"

Moon's and Sam's eyes were big with admiration; Jonas yawned. He'd seen Fred fight off a school of barracuda with no trouble at all when they were freshmen in high school (Moon had treated them to spring break in the Bahamas that March).

"But Jesus! They're so aggressive! Not to mention unpredictable. You do know that because they can tolerate shallows, and fresh water, that they're probably more dangerous to humans than great whites?"

"Thomas," Tennian said gently, "we're not human."

A short, embarrassed silence. Fred hid a smile and thought, *More Homo sapiens arrogance. Or is it chauvinism?*

"You are kind to be so concerned for our welfare," Wennd said, giving him a dazzling smile in which there were about a hundred razor-sharp teeth. At least, that's what it looked like. "We were perfectly fine. Not so much as a scratch on either of us."

"*That's* the stuff you should be telling *Time* and *Us Weekly*," Jonas said. " 'Gorgeous mermaids eat giant shark and live to tell the tale.' Get it? Tale?"

"They're too busy asking me about my freak hair," Fred said irritably. "And do you really want PETA and Greenpeace weighing in? They'll decide Undersea Folk are abusing natural resources and exploiting sharks and smoking kelp or what have you."

"You were right," Wennd said to Tennian. "She *is* wise."

This time, everyone was laughing—except for Fred, who glared.

"I just know a few things about fanatical surface dwellers," Fred said defensively. "That's all."

"So how did you arrive? Migrate? Whatever,"

Thomas asked. "It's not like the Indian Ocean is just a hop and a skip away from the Gulf."

Wennd gradually lost her nervousness and, as she talked with Thomas and even followed him outside to observe the grilling process, chatted amiably about her migratory habits, among other things.

Fred watched them getting along like super swell pals, wishing she didn't care and remembering wishing never helped anyone.

I've got to put him out of my head, is all. If he really loved me, he wouldn't keep chasing other mermaids. And if I really loved him, I wouldn't tolerate it. Or, at least I'd tell him I loved him.

But, oh, that felt like such a lie.

One thing was certain. If she married Artur, she could focus on an entirely new life. A fresh start . . . and she'd see to it that Moon could visit whenever she wanted. Shit, *she* would visit *Moon* whenever Moon wanted. Marrying the prince of the Undersea Folk didn't mean she had to turn her back on her life. It was just time for something new. That was all.

And why did that feel like another lie?

Twenty-five

{seahorse symbol}

Fred dove off the dock, automatically shifted to her tail, and went in search of lunch.

This was always accomplished quite easily. Although she was allergic to fish and shellfish, the ocean teemed with probably five times the plant life that dry land had. And she liked how quite a bit of it tasted. More than once she thought she should have gone into botany, because it would have been nice to know more about different underwater plants . . .

Time to mull that over later. She wanted to eat, and then she wanted to find Artur and tell him yes.

She found an underwater meadow and pulled up some stalks and leaves. They tasted mildly salty, almost bland (as opposed to some types of seaweed that fairly burst with flavor), and she ate until she felt about as svelte as a manatee.

Artur, she had been told, was in yet another meeting with his father, King Mekkam. Having thousands of their subjects "come out," so to speak, must require a lot of jawing back and forth between the king and his heir. But she knew he would head to her house when he finished and hoped to intercept him underwater, where they'd have a bit of privacy.

And behold! As though the thought had conjured him like a genie out of a bottle, here he came, swimming steadily toward her, his expression fixed in a worried frown.

Hi, Artur.

He kept swimming. He was less than fifteen yards away. What on earth could he be thinking about? Not that she thought she was a raving beauty or a phenomenal intellect, but he *had* made it clear he wanted her for his wife and wasn't interested in taking no for an answer.

In fact, she was used to fending him off, not seeking him out. Could this week get any more fucked up?

Artur! Hey!

He blinked, saw her, and smiled. *Ho, Little Rika. It pleases me to see you waiting for me.*

Eh, don't flatter yourself, I was hungry and my house is full of uninvited guests. Also, I walked in on Jonas and Dr. Barb doing it on my living-room carpet this morning. What a way to wake up! I had to Clorox my eyes.

Your life is difficult, Little Rika. The words were right, but she could feel he was only half listening.

She turned as he passed her and they swam in silence, side by side, for a few seconds. Then:

I wanted to let you know I've decided.

Hmmmm?

Oh, this was not happening. She'd been fretting and wondering and agonizing, practically, and now she was going to give him what she assumed was going to be the best news of his life (and yes, she was aware of how conceited that was) and he was barely paying attention.

What had her father said? *O irony, how she makes*

slaves of us all. Well, that was pretty damned close to the truth, wasn't it? That'll teach her to assume a man's just hanging around waiting for her to deign to marry him.

Artur, don't take this the wrong way, but will you snap the hell out of it? I'm trying to have a conversation!

He slowed and circled her, tail flexing powerfully, muscled arms behind his back. *I beg your leave, my Rika. My father and I have a problem . . . we think.*

Well, lay it on me. Maybe I can help.

He smiled at her. *For one who professes anger and irritation much of the time, you do a fine job hiding your generous nature.*

Flattery will get you, et cetera. She reached out and snatched at the base of his tail and managed to hang on—just. God, he was strong! She shook it, trying to get his full attention. *What's wrong?*

He instantly spun away and started heading back out to open sea; she managed to hang on—barely—to his back fins. She felt like a water-skier being hauled behind a speedboat with a jet engine.

My good father has noticed the disappearance of several of our people.

Really? You mean, they were supposed to be here

pretending this was HQ, and they never showed? Or—

Yes. That, and my father has simply lost contact with some of our people.

Fred mulled that one over, still hanging on to Artur's tail for dear life. Fish flashed by so quickly she couldn't identify the phylum, never mind the specific class.

She had discovered last year that Mekkam, as king, was the most powerful telepath of his people (in fact, the greatest telepaths were all members of the royal family . . . and her father had tried his coup in part because he was extraordinarily gifted in that area as well).

Mekkam could be in contact with any one of his subjects at any time. He could project his thoughts to *all* his subjects at any time. And, like all purebred Undersea Folk, his telepathy was just as powerful on land as it was beneath waves.

So it made sense that, if Undersea Folk were disappearing, he would be the first to notice.

Thus, all the frequent and secret meetings, she mused.

Indeed, Artur thought soberly.

Does he think they're dead? she worried.

We cannot be sure, which is why this matter is so

troubling. Usually, when one of us dies, my father can feel their death throes. He has felt none. Only—only— a blank silence where once there was a vibrant mind.

Jesus. She mulled that one over, troubled. *That's fairly sobering.*

Indeed.

So what's the plan?

We do not know.

That sucks. Maybe it's nothing. Maybe your dad's, uh . . . She coughed, sending up a stream of bubbles. . . . *getting old.*

Our telepathy gets stronger as we age. Not weaker.

That ruled out her theory of Undersea Folk Alzheimer's.

And her mind seized upon the fact he had so casually dropped: they get stronger? Stronger as they age? What other species on the planet got *more* powerful as they aged? She had to stifle the urge to kidnap Mekkam and do experiments on him.

Then a nasty thought hit her. *You don't think my father's up to his old tricks, do you?*

Silence.

Well. Do you?

Twenty-six

It seemed a long, long time before his answer came, and when it did, it was full of reluctance. *It has been suggested.*

Oh, that was subtle. Since Artur and Mekkam were the only ones in these super secret meetings, one of them had "suggested" it. Tricky, tricky, Artur.

Well. I guess I can't blame you. But he's only been here for a couple of days. How long have people been disappearing?

For half a year.

There you go. My dad's been too busy skulking in banishment to be disappearing unsuspecting Undersea Folk. Doncha think? Plus, he's been on land for most of the last thirty years. Hardly in a position to be ambushing unsuspecting mermaids.

There is another theory. Now Artur's reluctance was coming through so heavily, she could practically feel it crawling across her brain. *Perhaps . . . perhaps soldiers of the planet's land countries have been . . . doing things. Secret things.*

Okay. That's not altogether implausible, she admitted. Hell, she'd warned them, hadn't she? Her mother's species, in their own way, were even more bloodthirsty than Undersea Folk. At least the UF only killed to feed themselves or defend themselves. The same, unfortunately, could not be said for Homo sapiens.

I am relieved my theory has given no offense.

Tough to be offended by the truth . . . at least, this time. Frankly, it's pretty plausible that, I dunno, some secret government agency has been stealing Undersea Folk and doing experiments on them. How can we check it out?

I was hoping your friend Thomas might be of assistance.

How could he— She trailed off. Because of his money? No. Artur had tons of it. Because of his education? No. Fred was technically Artur's subject (though she'd eat a pound of sushi before bowing or referring to him as "my prince" or any of that other nonsense . . . she was an American, dammit!), and her background was as extensive as Thomas's . . . He didn't have to seek out a surface dweller. Then what—

It hit her. *His dad.*

Yes.

Thomas had been a navy brat. His father was some high-up mucky-muck in the U.S. Navy.

Do you think he would assist us?

Let's ask him.

Artur abruptly stopped swimming, but Fred's forward momentum shot her past his tail and into his arms.

I was mightily pleased to see you waiting for me.

And I was mightily pleased to have a fraction of your attention.

Only my father's displeasure and the welfare of my

people could blot you from my mind for the merest instant!

Daddy's boy.

Laughter. Laughter in her head. And with his arms around her, with that rollicking laughter echoing through her brain, she said before she could chicken out, *I've been thinking about it. I'll do it.*

Do what? he teased. *Insult my mighty intelligence? Throw Jonas into the pool yet again? Be disrespectful to your people's newsmakers?*

Reporters, she corrected automatically.

More laughter in her head. *Oh, no, you don't, Little Rika! I have watched much television. When there is no news, your "reporters" make the news.*

Can we debate the merits of modern journalism any other time but now? And no, numb fins, none of the above. What I meant was, I'll marry you. I'll be your wife.

Oh, Rika! He hugged her so hard that, if she'd had to breathe, she would have been in serious trouble. *Truly, you have made me the happiest man in the seas! Now, without doubt, you are she-who-will-be-my-wife.*

She snuggled into his embrace, hoping he wasn't

cracking her ribs. *You know, for a bunch of telepaths, you've got a remarkably bloated language. Try fiancée. Fee-on-say.*

It matters not, he said, and kissed her four miles out in the Gulf, forty feet below the waves, her green hair fanning out like an undeserved halo. Their hair was entwined, their arms were around each other, they were hungrily exploring each other's mouths, and Fred could feel the kiss all the way to the bottom of her tail.

There, she thought. *That's settled.*

Okay. Back to business.

Twenty-seven

🐚

"Awesome!" Jonas screamed, badly startling the saleswoman. "Princess Fred! Ohmigod! I can't stand it!"

"I can't stand it, either. Stop yelling." Fred, standing in front of the full-length mirror, scowled at her reflection. The dress was salmon-colored, had a mermaid skirt (doubtless Jonas's idea of a subtle joke) and a low-cut bodice and beading on the sleeves, and it clashed horribly with her hair. Odd. Jonas usually had much better taste than this. "And I'll bite your ears off if you make me buy this one."

"It wouldn't be in *that* color. Be serious. I told you: apple red. Dr. Barb's sister and cousin and you are all wearing apple red. Just like my tie and cummerbund are apple red—don't you remember?"

"No."

"Oh, look who I'm talking to."

She nodded in agreement. The small bridal shop was jammed with dresses of every size, shape, and color. An entire wall was devoted to white satin shoes. Another wall: clutch handbags in every style and color you could imagine. Playing over the speakers: *Trumpet Voluntary.* Well, that part wasn't so bad.

"So! When should I throw the party?"

"Party?" She had disappeared back into the dressing room to try on dress number four. She couldn't get dress number three off fast enough—she thought she heard a seam tear. Fuck it. "What party?"

"Your engagement party, dumbass! Let's see . . . we should probably have it at your rental house, since it's the—"

Fred groaned. Slipped number four over her head. Hmm. This one didn't entirely suck.

She stepped out. "Forget it. Artur and I have some Undersea Folk junk to look into. After the dust clears you can throw your stupid party."

"And don't forget, I'm planning your wedding."

"I wouldn't have it any other way," she said with complete and total sincerity.

"Now *that's* not bad," Jonas said, eyeing her up and down critically. She knew his taste was quite a bit better than hers and was happy to follow (fashion-wise) where he led. But she couldn't help agreeing. Strapless, with a tight-fitting bodice. A-line, with the skirt falling straight to the floor, just past her ankles. And the color was right: apple red. It made her hair seem even greener, almost the color of pine trees. And her eyes—the color did wonderful things to her eyes!

"We're done," Jonas told the saleslady. Then, to Fred, "See, see? Not even half an hour. You should trust me more often."

"I'm still digesting cake, you awful man. Never," she vowed, popping back into the dressing room to get back into her shorts, ratty T-shirt, and flip-flops.

"Behold," Jonas said mockingly as she stepped out. "The future queen of the Undersea Folk. At least they won't care if you don't wear a bra in the Black Sea."

"I hate bras," she muttered and stomped toward the front of the store to pay for the damned dress.

Twenty-eight

§

Thomas had left a note saying he was meeting some colleagues at the Florida Aquarium in Tampa Bay. Fred suggested to Artur that she drive them there and he readily agreed.

That was how she found out Artur hated being closed up in automobiles.

"For God's sake," she said, amazed, "you're perfectly safe."

Artur had his legs drawn up under his chin. His seat belt was tightened to the point of asphyxiation. He was trying not to huddle and failing. "All these metal boxes, hurtling by at ridiculous speeds. Madness, madness."

"You've never been in a car before?" She was dumbfounded. Then remembered this was a merman who lived at the bottom of the Black Sea. Okay. Not such a ridiculous idea, but still . . .

"No. I was on a train, once . . . in Boston. There was more room on the train. I could walk around on the train, although the king of the train did not like that."

She managed not to groan. "Don't tell me. You're claustrophobic."

"I don't know that term," he said, and she didn't think he'd ever been so white before.

"It means that you don't like small, enclosed spaces, um, mighty prince who conquers worlds and women with green hair."

He laughed hollowly, then cringed when a semi zipped by them, blaring its air horn. Fred flipped the driver the bird with both hands.

"Keep your hands on the steering device!"

"It's fine, see? I'm steering with my knee."

"Please don't," he moaned.

"Artur, for God's sake. You've taken on pirates,

great whites, survived a coup, and you're marrying me. I can't believe you're scared of anything, much less being in a car."

"I am not scared! I am . . . cautious."

She snorted. "Look, here's the exit. We're almost there, so don't pee your shorts just yet."

"You will show me the nearest body of water when we leave this place. I will swim back. You should join me."

"And abandon my rental car? Forget it. Think of the paperwork!"

"Paperwork?"

"I signed a contract," she said solemnly, trying not to laugh at him. "It's a very serious thing among surface dwellers, you know. Rental car contracts."

"I know of contracts. I would not want you to break your word. That would not befit my princess."

"And it would wreck my credit rating, too."

They pulled into the parking lot, picked up their visitor passes from a ticket seller, and went looking for Thomas.

Artur cheered up considerably once he was out of the compact car, and eyed the exhibits with great interest.

"Cheer up, brothers," he said softly, standing in front

of an exhibit of manta rays. "You are safe here and well fed. Were you free, you would be meat."

"Stop talking to the rays," Fred muttered, noticing the odd looks they were getting. She absolutely did not, *did not*, want to be recognized today. She and Artur had urgent business with Thomas. The business of her people.

My people, she mused. *Huh. Always before I've said my father's people. But they're just as much mine. Why didn't I see that before? Too busy hiding from myself, I guess. Poor Artur has no idea he's marrying a coward.*

"I could not help it," he said, sounding wounded. "They spoke to me first. Besides, you cannot speak to them on land, so it seemed rude to indulge in an ability you do not share."

Fred raised her eyebrows. That had come up before, her lack of telepathy on land. Artur had been almost embarrassed when he'd realized it. Was that going to be a problem for them?

She'd worry about it later, and for now led him away from the exhibit. She thought she heard someone say her name and she turned. But Thomas wasn't there.

They continued their search, separating so Artur could have a good long drink at the water fountain while Fred continued looking, eventually finding herself standing at the top of Shark Bay.

She peered in and saw sand tiger sharks, blacktips, zebra sharks. An impressively large sea turtle. Lionfish—big-time poisonous. Triggerfish. Dragon moray eels. Jellies. It really was—

"It's you! You're that mermaid I saw on TV!"

Stifling a groan, Fred turned. Several teenagers were standing behind her, all with gaping jaws and reeking of Stridex. "Hi," she said.

"Ohmigod! This is, like, rilly, rilly cool," one of the girls said, chewing a piece of gum roughly the size of her fist. "Like, you're a mermaid 'n' stuff! Cool!"

Fred mentally groaned. The girl sounded awfully like Madison, the twit intern at the New England Aquarium. An hour with Madison felt like a week; a week felt like a century. And Madison wore pink. Every day.

Even if she hadn't needed to spend her time as a press liaison, never having to lay eyes on Madison again would have been reason enough to quit her job.

"Ohmigod, it's really you!"

"Yeah, it is, but I can't really talk right—"

They were getting closer, pattering her with inane questions, and she automatically backed up.

"—how do you have sex with a tail?"

"—true your mom isn't a mermaid, so you're, like, both?"

"—howcum all the mermaids are rilly, rilly hot? It doesn't make sense. You mean there's not one fugly mermaid in the whole world? Not *one*?"

"Apparently not," one of the boys said, "and it's awesome!"

"Hey!" she snapped, feeling her thighs touch the rim at the top of the shark tank. "Back off, annoying adolescents, like that's not redundant."

But just then, worse luck, a classroom of teeming third-graders (she guessed, given their height and general grubbiness) burst onto the floor, pushing into the teenagers, who in turn pushed into Fred.

Who in turn toppled backward and fell into Shark Bay with a most undignified splash.

Twenty-nine

Getting oxygen was no problem, of course, but she couldn't swim without her tail. She couldn't even dog-paddle. She was as graceless in the water with legs as a penguin was on land.

So she flailed and wriggled and found herself upside down and batted aside the sea turtle and in general thrashed about like a dying seal.

She could see them.

She could see them *looking* at her, their noses

pressed against the glass, their mouths open as they jabbered excitedly.

And damned if she was going to shift to her tail in front of a bunch of Florida tourists. She wasn't a god-damned sideshow freak. She'd prefer the humiliation of graceless thrashing to giving the tourists a better show than Slappy the Seal.

She heard the hollow boom of water being displaced several feet above her head—someone diving into the tank. Ah, the final humiliation . . . rescued by a staff member and then hustled off the property by security. Must be Tuesday.

A strong hand seized her by the bicep and she felt herself being pulled toward the surface. She kicked, trying to help, and nearly got stung by a lionfish for her trouble. She had no idea if she was immune to their venom, so that was the end of the kicking.

They broke the surface and her rescuer took a deep breath.

"Hi, Thomas." She wiped limp green hair out of her eyes. No, that was seaweed. Yech. She tossed it behind her. "I've been looking everywhere for you."

He grinned at her and she noticed he hadn't taken off any of his clothes, just jumped in after her. "You thought I was in the shark tank? Come on."

He climbed up the ladder, stretched down a hand, and hauled her out of the tank.

Everyone was *looking*.

"Please," Fred said, and to her horror, she was near tears. "Please make them go away."

And she sank to the floor, miserable and drenched, and Thomas signaled someone and held her while the top of the tank was cleared of tourists.

Thirty

§

"Little Rika, what in the name of the king . . . ?"

She was still huddled in Thomas's arms like some pathetic romance-novel heroine, but the threatening tears had abated. Now all she wanted was a towel and a Cobb salad. Oh, and to pretend that the last five minutes hadn't happened.

Meanwhile, Artur was standing over them, hands on his hips, looking astonished and worried.

"What did you do?" he asked again.

"I fell in."

Artur squatted beside her and Thomas. "Clearly. But why in the world did you need Dr. Pearson to help you?"

Fred said nothing. She liked Artur fine, and was more than a little horny for him, and was looking forward to

(running away)

starting a new life in the Black Sea with him. But she couldn't tell him. He would never, ever understand. No one would ever under—

"Are you kidding?" Thomas snapped. "D'you think she wanted to nude up and shift to her tail in front of two hundred gaping tourists? Bad enough she can't go anywhere without being bugged. She's not a goddamned exhibit."

Aw, rats. Here came the tears again . . . tears of sheer gratitude.

She would have done anything for him then.

Anything at all.

"You are wrong." Artur's face—his expression bothered her—annoyed and disbelieving and something else, something she could almost put her finger on, something like

(shame)

embarrassment. For him? Or for her?

"You are wrong. My Rika cares not at all about what strangers think."

"He's right," she said quietly. "Thomas is, I mean. I didn't want to do that. Change in front of everybody."

Artur's brow furrowed. "But—but, Rika, why? Surely you're not shamed by your beautiful breasts and tail. Although," he added thoughtfully, "the nudity taboo surface dwellers insist on could be problematic, in addition to being quite silly. But you need not keep your hybrid nature a secret . . . Why, much of the country knows!"

"Look, I'm not a circus act, okay? They were all staring. I hate being stared at."

"I do not understand," he said flatly, mouth a grim slash. "It is not behavior that becomes one of the royal family."

"Well," she said. "I guess you're wrong about that one."

"Your behavior is senseless."

"Oh, shut your piehole, Artur!" she snapped, straightening. She realized that Thomas had been holding her the entire time Artur had been nagging her. The big lug didn't mind *that*, oh, no. But her tail shyness, that was the big problem.

For the first time, she truly understood the chasm that lay between her upbringing and his.

"I do not know what that means," he said flatly.

"It means get off my back. You're not the one being stopped on the street damned near every day. You're not the one who has to talk to insipid reporters every week. You're not the one on the cover of the *National Enquirer* with the so-flattering headline, 'Freak Mermaid Pregnant with Alien Baby.'"

"But you agreed to all this."

"I know! But sometimes it's a little much, that's all. You don't have to act like I stuck a knife into the worldwide morale of Undersea Folk."

"Uh, guys?" Thomas cleared his throat. "Listen, sorry to interrupt, but why don't we go somewhere a little more private? You said you needed to talk to me about a big problem with the Undersea Folk?"

Artur and Fred glared at each other for a few more charged seconds, then Artur cut his glance away and said, "You are correct, Thomas. We require your help."

"Aw." Thomas beamed. "The Team Supreme, together again."

"Let's hope nobody gets shot this time," Fred said sourly.

Thirty-one

"What do you mean, disappearing? They're not showing up where they're supposed to, or dead bodies are showing up, or what?"

Thomas had asked, very politely, if he could introduce her to his colleagues at the aquarium, and she had agreed. They seemed pleasant and professional, if a little wide-eyed, and asked no weird or deeply personal questions. For marine biologists face-to-face with a mermaid, Fred admired their self-control. She doubted she would have been able to equal it.

And then, after handshakes all around (and a formal presentation of a lifetime pass to the Florida Aquarium . . . Fred imagined it was their equivalent to the key to the city), they graciously withdrew, and the director said they could use her office, which is where they were now.

Artur was answering Thomas's question, and thank goodness, because Fred had forgotten what it was, so busy was she studying her lifetime aquarium pass (laminated!).

"My father cannot find them. They have disappeared from his mind."

"Bummer," Thomas commented. Fred knew he wasn't being flip. At least, he didn't *mean* to be flip. He just had no idea how to process the information at this time, but still felt he had to contribute to the conversation. "I know your dad's a pretty powerful telepath—"

"The most powerful," Artur corrected, not without pride. "It is that to be king. I, the heir apparent, am second most powerful."

"Whoa, wait," Fred interrupted. "So how come you didn't notice any of this?"

"Second powerful is still much less powerful than

my good father," Artur explained. "He is much, much older than I."

Fred nodded. Artur, though he didn't look it, was in his early fifties . . . fully two decades older than she was. Mekkam was over a hundred.

"Okay, so that answers that. Is it possible a bunch of them got—I don't know, the Undersea Folk equivalent of the bubonic plague and died all at once?"

Artur was already shaking his head. "No, Thomas. Were they dying, my king would feel it. They are simply . . . vanishing from his mind. Where once he could sense a vibrant, living being, there is now only silence."

"How many?"

"Four hundred seventy-eight."

Fred met Thomas's dismayed gaze and felt a similar expression on her own face. Almost five hundred! In less than a year!

"What—what do you want me to do? How can I help?"

Artur smiled for the first time in a long, long day. "Thomas, my people have a saying: we are made stronger by the honor our opponents hold. And at this moment you have made me strong indeed. We *do* need your help. We were hoping you might get in touch with your sire."

"Dad?" Thomas frowned, and then his dark eyes lit up. "Right! Navy Intelligence. You think the government's being sneaky, don't you?"

Artur looked at the floor, unwilling to offend a former opponent whom he had always respected. Fred had no such compunctions. "It's happened before, Thomas. It's been happening since there *was* a government."

Thomas ran a hand through his shaggy dark hair and nodded. "Yep, can't deny that one. Well, Dad's been retired, but he still holds the rank of captain. And he's got a whole bunch of buddies still on active duty. I'll call him right now." Thomas laughed. "He'll be thrilled his sissy son needs his help."

Fred's mouth fell open. "Whaaaaat? The captain thinks Switchblade Pearson is a sissy?"

"I didn't go into the military," he said simply.

"I regret asking you to do anything that will put any strain on your relationship with your sire."

"Forget about it, Artur. This is a shitload more important than Dad and me."

"I thank you."

"But you're a doctor," Fred said, dumbfounded. "And a Ph.D.! And you've got street smarts and you designed the URV and you're a bestselling author and—sissy?"

Thomas grinned. "Bestselling *romance* author, don't forget."

Fred made a mental note to slug Captain Pearson when she met him. Who *wouldn't* want their kid to be so brilliant he could turn his back on medicine and study an entirely new field? And kick ass in *both* fields? Military-minded moron.

"Well, thanks. Should we go to him, or will he come down here?"

"I happen to know that since retirement he's been bored out of his tits."

"Pardon?" Artur asked.

"Never mind. He'll come down here. He'll pretend it's a huge inconvenience, but he'll be here. And then I guess we'll try to get to the bottom of this." Thomas lost his habitual wiseass expression and sobered. "I hope your people aren't dead, Artur. I'll do everything I can to help you find them."

They shook hands, surface-dweller style.

Thirty-two

Later, Fred was sitting thoughtfully by the pool. The sun had gone down about an hour ago and she had a lot to think about. Thank goodness she finally had a little bit of—

"Okay, that's enough sulking, Fish Face. What's the matter?"

Jonas. Of course. Her mouth said, "Die painfully, Jonas, and preferably quietly." Her mind said, *Thank God. I really need to talk to him. He'll understand and he'll tease me and he won't judge and then I'll feel better. God, if you're paying any attention at all up there, thank you so much for dropping Jonas in my life when we were in elementary school.*

"C'mon," he was coaxing. "Spill."

"Don't you have bouquets to sniff or china to pick out?"

"Done and done . . . Barb and I registered today. Feel free to buy us many grossly expensive gifts at Macy's, Crate and Barrel, and Tar-jhay."

"It's Target, numb wad, and I've got up until a year after the wedding to cough up a gift."

"You *did* read that copy of Miss Manners I left in your room!"

"Shut up." She sighed, cupping her chin in her hand. She was sitting on a lawn chair and staring into the pool. "Something bad happened today."

"You wore white after Labor Day?"

"Hilarious. I fell into the shark tank at the aquarium."

Jonas coughed, except it sounded oddly like a muffled laugh. "Oh?" he managed.

"Yeah, and never mind how it happened. The thing is, everybody was staring at me. And I didn't—"

"—want to shift to your tail in front of the whole damn aquarium, sure. I get it."

"Artur didn't."

"Oh. You guys have a fight?"

"Not really. It's just—he didn't get it at all. He was almost . . . I had the impression . . . I felt like he was sort of . . ."

"Ashamed of you?" Jonas asked quietly, sitting cross-legged at her feet.

"Well. Yeah."

"He's under some pressure," Jonas reminded her. "The missing mermaids and all, like you were telling me."

"Yeah."

"And he wants to marry you *because* you do weird-ass stuff like flailing around in a tank in your flip-flops instead of stripping to your birthday suit and growing a tail. You think you're the only engaged couple who come from radically different backgrounds?"

"I didn't think about it like that," she admitted.

" 'Cuz you're stupid," he informed her cheerfully.

"Thanks so much."

"So what was Thomas doing while you guys were working out radical cultural differences?"

"Uh. Holding me."

Jonas groaned and stretched out on the concrete. He lay there, corpse-like, for a few seconds, then propped himself up on an elbow and went into scold mode. "Fred, Fred, Fred! You've made your choice. You strung both of them along for . . . what? Two years? And now you're engaged . . . to—are you listening?—Artur! Enough with the dancing! Ow, I think I just scraped all the skin off my elbow."

"I didn't string them along," she protested, stung. "They're the ones who kept disappearing. At least Artur made it clear from day one that he wanted to marry me."

"Ahaaaaaa!" he yowled. "What you meant is, *Thomas* kept disappearing on you. So you picked Artur."

"Yes, and my choice had nothing to do with the fact that he loves me and will make me a princess and show me things I could never, ever have discovered on my own."

Jonas held up his hands, as if he were being robbed.

"Fair enough. I'm not arguing any of that stuff. But my point is, you made your choice. So enough with the wishy-washy bullshit."

"Artur was embarrassed. But Thomas pulled me out of the tank. He jumped right in and hauled me out. And he *knew* why I didn't pop my tail."

"Big surprise, you were raised by surface dwellers and another surface dweller gets you. *I* get you. It doesn't mean Artur's embarrassed, or ashamed, or regretting anything. You've got years to work all this crap out. Why is it bothering you so much tonight?"

"I don't know. I absolutely don't. It's been a weird week."

Massive understatement.

"And you've got another weird-ass mystery to solve. You're the Daphne to their Shaggy and Fred."

"The hell! I'm Velma, dammit."

"And you're on television and in papers and you hate the attention."

"So?"

"So. Give Artur a break. You're not exactly at your best right now. And he was *still* glad when you said yes."

"That's true."

Jonas leaned over and gave her a friendly slap on the leg. "See? All is well when you listen to your uncle Jonas."

"Just when I thought you couldn't get any creepier."

"You can't imagine my levels of creepiness. Now if you'll excuse me, I'm going upstairs to bone your boss."

Fred shut her eyes, but the awful images wouldn't disappear.

Thirty-three

Fred didn't dare go in the house, which was a shame, because the mosquitoes were a real bitch tonight. But Jonas and Dr. Barb could get pretty loud. She prayed they were at least doing it in their bedroom.

"Fredrika?"

She turned and looked. Her father had stepped out onto the patio. "Oh. Hi, Farrem. What's up?"

"Nothing is up. Only . . ." He hesitated. She had the odd feeling he was shy, or embarrassed. "I have not had the chance to speak with you in private. Do you mind?"

"Mind? I'd love the distraction, *believe* me. Have a seat. Hope you brought a can of Off!"

He chuckled. "You poor thing! Mosquitoes don't like how Undersea Folk taste. What an awful heritage to inherit from your lady mother."

"Thank God!" Fred exclaimed. "A UF who understands a surface-dweller reference. Usually I get a blank stare."

Farrem's laughter cut off abruptly. "Yes, I know that Off! is an insect repellant. I know many things about the surface world, as I have had to spend much time here."

"Uh. Yeah. Sorry. Didn't mean to bring the party down."

He sat in the patio chair beside her. "You did not. I will carry my shame for the rest of my days, and deservedly so; your comments have no effect on what I have done. But there have been compensations for banishment. I am sitting beside one of them."

"Aw," Fred teased. "I'm blushing."

"It is too dark for me to tell," he replied.

"Farrem, can I ask you something?"

"Because I was arrogant and thought my wishes

were more important than sparing lives. Because I was cruel and foolish."

"Um. I was going to ask where you've been living all these years."

"Oh! Awkward," he said wryly, and Fred laughed again. Damn! It was great to talk to someone who didn't sound stilted, or from another

(species)

country.

"I have seen much of the planet. In my despair, I traveled much of the world during my first decade of banishment . . . starting, of course, with the East Coast of this country. Specifically, Massachusetts."

"Specifically, Cape Cod," Fred said dryly, knowing well that she was conceived on one of the beaches there.

"Indeed! My encounter with your lady mother was the one thing that kept me from despair. I had forgotten a very basic fact. Although my own people despised me, there were many people who would not know of my shame. She was kindness itself. She . . . saved me."

Fred said nothing, but her thoughts were awhirl. She and Jonas had long ago agreed never to tell Moon that

Farrem had only taken her out of despair, had come ashore because he had, literally, nowhere else to go. But Fred was having second thoughts.

She . . . saved me.

Moon deserved to know the wonderful thing she had done for a man she didn't know.

How often, Fred mused, had she taken her mother's generous nature for granted?

Since day one, of course. Did anyone ever *really* appreciate their mom?

Farrem had been silent while she pondered these things, and when he continued, it was in a low voice. "I had been planning my own destruction. I had planned to find land, get as far from water as I could, and die by dehydration."

"Jesus!"

"It is very difficult," he said simply, "for one of our kind to kill themselves. I supposed I could have let myself be eaten by a great white. Messy, though, and quite painful. But!" He sounded more brisk. Slightly more cheery, thank God. "Your lady mother made me rethink my course of action. So I went a'traveling. I saw many things."

"How did you—you know . . . Live? Make money? Whatever?"

"At first, I caught and sold fish at various coastal markets. When I wound up in Tokyo, I realized how very expensive sushi quality fish are—tuna, whitefish, squid—"

"Yerrggh! Stop, you'll make me barf."

"What?"

"I'm allergic."

"Stop that. You are teasing me."

"I'm absolutely not. I can't eat any kind of fish."

Her father went into gales of laughter at her confession. Most Undersea Folk did. They thought her hideous affliction was hilarious. "Oh! Oh, in the king's name! A child of mine, allergic!"

"I'm thrilled you're getting such a kick out of this."

"I do beg your pardon, Fredrika. But it *is* funny. I noticed you have your mother's teeth; it's actually quite a good thing you can't eat fish. Frankly, you don't have the dentition for it."

"Good point. So, you were in Tokyo . . ."

"And eventually made enough money to buy a fishing boat. And due to my . . . ah . . . affinity with the sea—"

"You always knew where to find the fish!"

"Just so."

"How many boats," she asked slyly, "do you have now?"

"Twenty-two. And homes in Tokyo, Greenland, and Perth."

She laughed. "Perth, Australia? Get out of town!"

"I assure you, I will, and quite soon. I also," he went on with what she felt was justifiable pride, "supervise a staff of several hundred."

"So you did sort of get your own kingdom, after all."

"I had not thought of it that way. You are wise for one so young, Fredrika."

"I s'pose you're going to tell me you're eighty years old or whatever— Never mind, I don't want to know. Tokyo, Greenland, and Perth, hmm? Lots of water in those areas."

"Not to mention saltwater pools on all my properties."

"That's great, Farrem." She meant it. She was proud of him, despite what he had done. At least he'd learned. He hadn't let it get him down and, by God, he'd grown. Made something of himself. She'd known plenty of humans who couldn't let go of the past. Who *wallowed* in the past.

Shit, who *hadn't* fucked up when they were younger?

"I think you did really well in a pretty difficult situation. And I'm glad you found me. I admit, I've been curious about you."

"And I, once I saw your picture, about you. You are the only hybrid I have ever known. It never occurred to me that I might have left your lady mother in pup. I am embarrassed to say I never came back to check on her."

"Well, like you said. You couldn't have known. Frankly, I'm amazed myself—two species usually can't mate successfully. You don't see any tiger/monkeys or seal/dolphins around."

"Ah . . . no. I sometimes wonder," he mused, "if the fool things I did in my youth had a purpose. One beyond my selfish desires. Because they led to you. And look what you have done, for your mother's people and for mine. You have changed . . . everything. Everything."

"Oh, it wasn't me," Fred said, startled and embarrassed. "The king's the one who said his subjects could choose to show themselves or not. I'm just . . . trying to help with the transition."

"And I am certain you had nothing at all to do with that decision," he said slyly, and she laughed.

"You should hang around," she said. "You're good for my ego."

"That is part of why I wanted to speak with you. I dare not hang around. At least, not much longer. I will not jeopardize your standing among my people. We are an old race, and a stubborn one. And we blame the children for the deeds of their parents. Illogical, yes, but part of who we are. Surely you have already run into prejudice because I am your sire."

"Nothing I can't handle."

"You are kind. But if you are to rule, you must not have me forever reminding our people of the terrible danger I once placed us all in."

"Danger—for them?"

"I was never meant to be king," he said simply. "If I had succeeded in my foolishness, all of our people could have been in jeopardy. No, Mekkam's line has been ruling us for a reason. I was too stupid in my youth to understand such things."

"Well. Uh." Fred cleared her throat. "Why did you think you should take over?"

"I once thought that just because your father, and grandfather, and great-grandfather had been king, that didn't mean that *you* should be king. I thought it was more about ambition, and ability, than heredity."

"You must have been studying the Windsors," Fred said dryly. "Because you're sure not alone in that. But that's neither here nor there—you don't think so anymore?"

He laughed. "I was defeated, was I not? That in itself proved me wrong. But what it took me thirty years to understand was that—and this is what you might call my 'duh' moment—Artur's line rules *because* their formidable telepathy is hereditary. It is through that ability that he safeguards our people. I had no right to attempt to usurp him."

"The way I heard the story is, you're pretty formidable yourself. In the telepathy area, that is."

"That was both my gift and my curse, yes."

She understood: if not for his power, he never would have tried the coup; he never would have been banished.

"That must be amazing. I can only hear the UF and fish and such when I'm in water, with my tail."

He frowned and cocked his head. "Beg your pardon?"

"I can't talk to Undersea Folk on land like purebreds can. I can't hear fish on land, sense them—nothing like that."

"You—you're mind blind when you have legs?" He was trying hard not to sound horrified, and failing.

"Hey, it's okay, Farrem. I've always felt

(like a freak)

different because I could hear fish. I didn't even know about UF telepathy until I met Artur. So I never knew what I was missing. It doesn't bother me."

He was—why was he looking at her so strangely?

"Fredrika," he said quietly, and knelt by the pool, and dipped his finger in the water, and drew some odd, complicated symbols on the dry cement, "can you tell me what this word is?"

She stared at the squiggles and lines. "It's a word? It looks like abstract art to me."

He sat back on his haunches, and why in the world did he look so *sad*?

"What's wrong?" she asked, nearly gasped. Suddenly it was hard to get a breath. "You look—what's wrong with me?"

"This is your name in our language," he said quietly,

gently. "You can only speak our language in your mind, in water."

"I can't speak your language at all! When I talk to fish and—and Artur and Tennian and those guys, we're speaking English."

"You are not. You are speaking the ancient language of all the seas, the tongue that was common long before a fish who wanted to be a man crawled out of the ocean and grew lungs. We—the Undersea Folk—we know it through ancestral memories. We are all born knowing it. When you communicate with us telepathically, you are speaking our ancient tongue. It cannot be taught; you must have the memories for it, the ancient memories. But your mother's blood is strong in you, and—it's not just your teeth, daughter."

"What—I—what?"

"You can never read our legends. You can never communicate with us on land in our language. We can learn English . . . or French . . . or Italian. Those chatterings are ludicrously simple compared to the much older language of the sea. That is why we can speak with you on land. But you never can speak our tongue, hear those thoughts, read those stories, learn those legends. And you might pass on that—that surface-dweller trait—" My, how diplomatic he was! "You might pass that on to any children you give the prince."

Fred sat, frozen, and digested everything he had told her. "Why—why didn't Tennian tell me? Why didn't Artur?"

"I suspect," he said softly, "they could not bear to."

"Well." She mulled the shock of the day over for a minute or two. "That explains why Artur acts so weird whenever I do an un-mermaid-like thing."

"With all respect to the prince, your—ah—genetic inability to understand our language presents a considerable handicap." Farrem paused, then added, "He must love you a great deal to wish you for his queen."

"Yes," she said sharply, "he managed to overcome his repugnance at the thought of my gross defect." Which wasn't far from the truth. Certainly when Artur had first realized her limits, he and Tennian had acted as if she'd been born blind or something. Sad, and sympathetic, and slightly weirded out. It had been—

"Forgive me. I—I was thoughtless and—and cruel."

She waved a hand. "No, no. It's just—the shock, is

all. And the thing is, I think my, um, handicap or what-have-you bothers him more than he lets on."

"It matters not, if he loves you, and he must—a great deal! I truly meant no offense. I was surprised. I naturally assumed one of my blood— Oh, Fredrika," he said sadly. "I am so very sorry."

"For God's sake, what are we, at a wake? I told you, it's fine."

But was it?

She was amazed that Artur would chance her polluting the royal family with—to be brutally honest—surface-dweller retardation. What good was a future king *who couldn't speak or read the fucking language*?

Did Artur perhaps feel that, after pursuing her for two years, he could not back down? Could not take back his proposal when she told him she'd marry him?

"It's fine," she repeated stubbornly.

"Then you are truly of my blood, Fredrika, because we have both acquitted ourselves in difficult situations."

"If you say so. Listen, I get your remorse and everything, and I probably wouldn't be the only one. Maybe if some of the, uh, old guard heard you talking like that, they might—"

She quit when he laughed.

"All right, maybe that's naïve. But here's something you might not know—people from my generation don't blame me for what you did. They weren't around for what you did. My friend Tennian doesn't blame me, and her friend Wennd doesn't, either—it's a story to them and that's all."

"Wennd?"

"Oh, just the most beautiful woman in the world. Don't get me started. Anyway, that's the generation I'll be ruling. Maybe I could un-banish you when I become queen."

He looked at her for a long time. Finally he said, "You are your mother's daughter. Which is more than I deserve. I will not hold you to what you just said, and I will not repeat it, ever, because I would not jeopardize your throne for anything. But I will never forget it."

He leaned in. Touched her hair. Turned.

Left.

Thirty-four

🦑

Jonas opened the door to the guest room and stepped inside. His ridiculously hot fiancée, Barb, was barefoot, in her linen capris and a navy blue bra. Her blond hair was out of its habitual ponytail and streaming past her shoulders. She was looking at herself critically in the mirror, her almond-shaped brown eyes narrowed in concentration.

"What's up, sexy?"

"I've decided you're marrying a crone."

He groaned and flopped, face-first, onto the bed.

Then he rolled over so he could ogle her. "Not this again, Barb. I swear, you got progressively more neurotic about your age the moment we got engaged."

"A crone," she repeated, examining her laugh lines.

"Fifteen years, Barb. BFD."

"What?"

"Big. Fucking. Deal."

"You kids and your slang," she teased.

He wasn't about to be diverted. "So what if you're older than me? You're *supposed* to be older, remember? As in, I'm not attracted to women my own age? I've got the hot schoolteacher/older woman fetish? Any of this ringing a bell?"

"Some of it," she admitted and smiled at him.

"I wanted you the second I saw you in that starchy lab coat, all strict and hot and hot."

"You said hot twice."

"Well. You're twice as hot as anybody else."

She laughed at him. "You can say that with a straight face, surrounded by all these ridiculously beautiful mermaids?"

"What can I say?" He sighed. "Love is blind."

"Mmmm." She stripped off her pants and hung them

neatly over the chair before the mirror. "Did you get a chance to talk to Dr. Bimm?"

"Barb, since you're marrying her best friend, and since she keeps trying to quit and thus doesn't consider herself your employee anymore, I think you can start calling her Fred."

"She will not quit. I will never allow her to quit," she said firmly. "Even before I knew of her—ah—her unique heritage, she was the finest employee I ever had. She is on a leave of absence. She has *not* quit."

Jonas wondered why he surrounded himself with the most stubborn women on the planet.

Oh. Right. Because they were super damned sexy.

"I love how you're all formal and stuff."

"And I love how you're not." She smiled at him in the mirror. "But back to Dr. Bimm. Did you get a chance to talk with her?"

"Yeah. She had a rough day. All kinds of shit going on. I think I cheered her up a little. Or at least made her feel better."

"Can I help?"

"I don't think so, hon. She and Thomas and Artur

have some sort of plan to fix the problem of the year, and the three of them make a good team."

"So my late ex-husband will attest," she said dryly. Then: "I worry about the stress she's under." She disappeared into the bathroom and Jonas heard running water. "Shhhzz gnnn mmm mmmms."

"Spit out the toothpaste and try again, hon."

Spitting. Rinsing. Then: "She's got too many problems. It's not fair that so much should be on her shoulders, and in such a short time."

"Haven't you been paying attention, gorgeous? We don't live in a fair world. Anybody who says different is selling something."

"You stole that," Barb accused, "from *The Princess Bride*."

"Sure I did. But it doesn't make it less true."

Barb came out of the bathroom naked. She sighed and said, "I wish Dr. Bimm was the type of person who would ask for help."

"What?"

"I said, I wish— Jonas, I know that look."

He'd gotten off the bed and was battling with his belt. "What look?"

"Your I-must-be-sexually-satisfied-right-now look. And I *said*, I wish Dr. Bimm was the type of—"

"Please. Please stop talking about Fred. It'll ruin everything. The only way it could be less sexy is if you starting talking about one of my aunts." He managed to shove down his jeans and underwear, then nearly tripped as he tried to close in on Barb. "Fred's fine. Hey, you don't know where I can find a hot older woman to play stern schoolteacher, do you?"

Barb had a hand over her mouth, trying in vain to stifle her giggles. "You're going to fall and give yourself a concussion."

"A small price to pay," he said, and then he *did* trip, falling into her. She held him for a moment, then toppled to the rug beneath his greater height and weight. She groaned as the breath whooshed out of her lungs. "Barb? You okay?"

"You're going to pay for that," she said, twining her fingers in his hair and wrenching his mouth toward hers.

"I certainly hope so," he murmured and kissed her, cupping her right breast as he did so. "For hours, I hope."

"That's more up to you than me," she said into his mouth, then squealed as he pinched her.

Thirty-five

§

Thomas Pearson, M.D., Ph.D., and BIHSY-
DWTMW (Boy In High School You Didn't Want To
Mess With), pulled up to Fred's opulent rental house

(man, this place really isn't her)

and killed the engine. As if seeing Fred wasn't stressful enough, today he had to contend with the captain.
Man, if anybody but Fred had asked . . .

It was so stressful, in fact, that he tended to leave
Fred's place at dawn and sulk in the Starbucks down the
street. And he didn't have a key, which meant waking

the house when he returned. Maybe Fred would answer, possibly nude . . .

He tried to shove that out of his mind as he approached the front door. Fred wasn't his, was never his, would never be his. She was going to marry Artur, and who could blame her?

Artur could show her a world he never, ever could. The guy was a prince, for God's sake. And could know a side of Fred that Thomas could never relate to—Fred was, after all, only *half* human. She would be cheating herself and her father's heritage by starting a relationship with plain ordinary human Dr. Pearson, and Thomas knew that perfectly well.

Also, he was a fucking coward.

He rapped on the door.

Yep, a coward, a yellow-belly asshole, most definitely, yes, sir, and yes, ma'am, no argument, no question. How many times had he scuttled out of town because he knew he wasn't good enough for her? And when Artur moved in, how many times had Thomas fled the fucking *country* so he wouldn't have to watch the courtship close up? Knowing, always knowing, that whether he stayed or left, the end result would have been the same.

(but you didn't even try you didn't even)

He ignored the irritating inner voice. His father's voice, so quick to point out shortcomings, so quick to spot weakness.

Jesus, he'd even tried to substitute Tennian for her, and that had worked for about eight whole seconds. It was stupid of him and horribly unfair to Tennian, and it hadn't taken him long at all (eight seconds, in fact) to determine that he and Tennian would only, always be friends. *Just* friends. To her credit, Tennian had never tried to push it further

(Why would she? When she, like Fred, could have any man?)

and he was grateful for that.

He'd been gone on Fred even before he knew she was a mermaid—sorry, Undersea Folk. If Artur hadn't killed the sadistic fuck who'd shot her, he would have taken care of it himself. As it was, jamming his knife into her shoulder to get the bullet out was the hardest thing he'd ever had to do.

So hard, in fact, that he had avoided her more or less regularly ever since. Because if he felt that way on such short acquaintance, how might he feel—how much would it hurt—to fall even *more* in love? What if he had to hurt her *again* to save her?

He still had nightmares about it. Fred, shot. Artur, holding her down so he could dig out the bullet. Fred, screaming.

Screaming.

He pounded harder. That was no way to be thinking. That was past, it was done, and he was here now because she needed his help and, by God, he was going to do everything he could to—

A yawning Jonas opened the door. "What? D'you know what time it is? Jeez."

"It's oh-eight-twenty," Thomas replied, "and the captain will be here at oh-eight-thirty."

"Seriously?"

"You can set your fucking watch," he said glumly. "And good morning to you, too."

"Not a morning person, so kindly drop dead and disintegrate into a thousand tiny pieces." Jonas stepped back so Thomas could enter.

Thomas liked Jonas a lot. In another world—a world where he could be around Fred every day without destroying himself or ruining her life—they could have been best friends. Jonas did not take himself at all seriously, a quality Thomas greatly admired. He also loved Fred—a quality Thomas could relate to.

But, even though they weren't best friends, he was fond enough of the guy to poke him in the gut as he passed him.

"Keep your hands off my rock-hard abs, shithead," Jonas said warmly.

"Rock hard? For a second I mistook you for the Pillsbury Doughboy. Hee-*hee*!"

"Lies," Jonas yawned, "from a teeny, envious mind."

That was a little too close to the truth, even if Jonas didn't know it. "Is Fred up?"

"Up and in the pool since oh-God-thirty this morning. She's been sulking on the bottom of the deep end for the last hour or so."

"Great." Oh, Lord, she would be in her tail, her glorious, gorgeous, amazing tail, and her unbelievably fine tits would be bare and her taut stomach would—"Uh, could I have some coffee?" *To throw in my face so I can keep my mind on business?*

"In the kitchen." Jonas stretched. He was wearing Opus the Penguin pajama bottoms and nothing else.

"I guess I better get dressed if your dad's on the way."

"Why? You don't have to be there."

"What? And miss meeting The Thing That Spawned Thomas Pearson? No chance, pal."

Thomas laughed. His father would assume, as nearly everyone did, that Jonas was gay. When, in fact, Jonas was merely the most metrosexual fellow on the planet. Well, that was fine. Anything that irritated the captain was fine.

"Hey, will you give me an address where you actually pick up mail?" Jonas asked on his way back up the stairs. "We have no idea where to send the wedding invitation."

"Send it care of my publisher," he suggested. A navy brat, Thomas felt itchy if he was in the same place more than nine months. Funny, since when he was a kid he swore he'd pick one spot and never move again. He'd moved eighteen times since he became the legal drinking age. "They can always track me down. I'll e-mail you their address."

"Great, Priscilla." Jonas yawned and continued up the stairs. "See if you can haul Fred out of the pool, will ya? And Artur's gonna be here any minute."

"No doubt," he muttered and went through the sliding door and down the stairs to the pool.

Thirty-six

Yup, there she was, at the bottom of the pool. But she wasn't sulking in the deep end. She was swimming back and forth, back and forth; it was almost hypnotic. She was so strong that it took just a few flicks of her tail to carom to the other end of the pool—which was Olympic-sized. Facedown. Back and forth. Flick. Flick. Turn. Back and forth.

She was thinking about something. Thinking hard. He almost hated to disturb her, but the captain would need to talk to her and Artur.

He knelt and lightly slapped his palm on the surface of the water. He could barely hear the splash, but she flipped over at once, spotted him, and shot to the surface.

"Morning."

"Hi," he replied, then realized his voice had actually cracked. Christ, he always felt sixteen years old when he was around her. He coughed. "Hi," he said in a much more baritone-esque tone.

She bobbed out of the water, crossed her forearms on the cement, and rested her chin on her left wrist. "Say. I never thanked you. For yesterday, at the aquarium."

"No big."

"It was a 'big.' To me."

He shrugged. "Can't blame you for not wanting to show your boobs to a bunch of tourists, although, if I can offer a professional medical opinion, they're probably the third-finest set in the country."

"Third?" she cried with mock outrage, and splashed him. "You dog. How much research have you done in this field, exactly?"

"I almost went into plastic surgery," he lied, and grinned down at her. "Listen, sorry to interrupt your ruminating—"

"Oooh, someone's been using Word a Day toilet paper again."

"Off my back, *doctor*. The Captain's going to be here any minute."

She was staring at him thoughtfully and he noticed, again, that her eyes were the color of creamy jade. He had heard her refer to them as "the hideous tinge of Brussels sprouts" and wondered, for the zillionth time, why beautiful women never knew they were beautiful.

"You did it again," she said after a long moment.

Tell me, tell me she's not reading my mind.

"Did what?" he asked with feigned lightness.

"Called your dad 'captain.' I call my dad Farrem, but I've known him less than a week."

Thomas shrugged and started to stand. Quicker than thought—than his eyes could even track—one of her hands shot out and grasped his wrist with the strength that never, ever failed to surprise him.

She could snap my wrist without breaking a sweat. But she would never. And she doesn't even know how marvelous that makes her on a planet where you can get knifed for the five-dollar bill in your pocket.

Artur will tell her, he tried to comfort himself. *He'll tell her how great she is every day.*

"I didn't realize," she admitted. "When Artur and I thought about asking you to call your dad. I didn't know you didn't have a, um, loving-type relationship."

He shrugged. "How could you?"

"But you called him anyway."

"Sure."

She shook her head and smiled and released his wrist. Thank God, because his fingers were starting to lose all sensation. "You're too good, Thomas. You were a dope to let Tennian go."

"There was never anything to let her out of," he explained (again). "Ask her."

"No chance . . . she might bring that Wennd girl around again."

"Oh, my God," he said, staring up at the sky. "The eyes. The hair. Could you believe it?"

"I know! I felt like El Frumpo just being in the same room with her. Did you believe how shy she was? She was actually nervous to meet us. Us! And we're completely harmless!"

Thomas, who had a somewhat more objective view of Fred and her gang, said nothing.

"Speaking of difficult fathers, I had a really cool conversation with mine," she said and laid it out for him in about five minutes.

"So he got rich? He owns a fleet? And multiple houses on land?" Thomas shook his head, smiling. "Not bad for the traitor of his people."

"Tell me. And he's getting out of town pretty soon, too. He's worried that him being around will be a constant goad to the old guard. That it'll threaten my throne, if you can believe it."

"Thirty years is a long sentence."

"And it's not over yet. He's still banished from Undersea Folk society. But even the king couldn't banish him from land. But I think you're forgetting something. Thirty years is nothing to a UF. It's a Sunday afternoon. It's a sick day."

"Point," he admitted. He glanced at his watch, and she noticed.

"All right, I'm coming." She started to heave herself up and Thomas handed her the robe on the lawn chair, politely (and reluctantly) averting his eyes as he did so. He'd seen her breasts a few times, but only when she had a tail. "I better throw some clothes on before 'the captain' gets here."

"That would be nice," he agreed.

Thirty-seven

Captain Pearson pulled up to the unbelievably showy mini-mansion and shut off the car. He glanced at his watch: oh-eight-thirty.

He got out. Marched up the walk. Rapped precisely three times on the front door, automatically making sure his slacks and shirt were neat, his shoes shined. His hair, military short, needed no adjustment, despite the mild breeze.

His boy had called and he had come.

The boy never called.

The boy was all he had of his dear wife, cruelly snatched away by breast cancer forty-two months and eighteen days ago.

The boy did not like him and was quite correct to feel that way. He, Capt. James T. Pearson (ret.), decorated veteran of the Vietnam conflict, had been a shit father.

He hoped to have a chance to make up for the past. For his carelessness and close-mindedness and cruel comments. Because his wife had been right all along, and he was just a stubborn old man who had made too many mistakes.

The door opened, and there he stood. His boy, tall and strong and handsome—so handsome! With (oh, God) his mother's eyes staring out at him.

Book smart, too, plenty smart—a doctor! Two kinds of doctor, actually. And he wrote silly stories for the fun of it and even though it was just a hobby, the boy had turned it into a seven-figure-a-year income. In his spare time! The captain had tried to read one of the stories and didn't care for it, but plenty of other people sure seemed to. He had researched the romance—what did they call it? The romance genre. He'd been astounded to discover it was a billion-dollar industry . . . and his boy had cleverly tapped into it.

Whenever he had to fly somewhere, he always checked the airport bookstores and was always pleased to find one or more of the boy's stories on a shelf.

Once, it had seemed so vitally important that the boy serve his country. It seemed like a slap in America's face when the boy had gotten a scholarship and gone to medical school. He had not spoken to the boy for many years.

He had thought the boy frivolous and silly and maybe, maybe even a coward.

He was a stupid old man.

"Hello, Captain."

And, even though he was stupid, he would never show the boy how much it hurt to be called captain by the only son he would ever have . . . the only living reminder of his wife. Because he had it coming, all that and more.

How arrogant he had been to think that he would never have to pay for his sins. That the past didn't have teeth.

"Good morning, Thomas. May I come in?"

"Yes, sir."

The captain followed the boy into a large room that seemed to be a combination kitchen/dining room/living room. An exuberant blond fellow was fairly bouncing down the stairs, heading straight for them.

"Hey, hi there!" The man—compact and muscular, with a friendly smile—extended a hand. "I'm Jonas Carrey, I'm a friend of your son's. It's great to meet you."

The captain shook hands. "Hello, Mr. Carrey. I'm James Pearson."

"So, you really unleashed the thing that is Thomas upon the world? And you own up to it and everything?"

The captain was startled into laughter and, from the look on the boy's face, he wasn't the only one who was startled. "Yes, Mr. Carrey. I freely admit to it. He is my son. Fortunately, he takes after his mother."

The boy raised his eyebrows.

"It's Jonas, Captain Pearson. Thomas said you earned about a thousand medals in Vietnam, and led men into battle, and you were always the last one in retreat, and you saved a whole bunch of soldiers." Mr. Carrey actually gasped for breath after this recitation.

The captain, shocked, glanced at the boy, who

shrugged. He had no idea Thomas *ever* spoke of him, much less in complimentary terms he did not deserve.

"I did what I could for my country," he replied carefully. "That's the best any soldier can hope for."

"Spoken like a man used to kicking ass. I like you, Captain Pearson, despite the fact that you fathered Thomas, here, who's irritating in almost as many ways as my friend Fred. If you're in town long enough, you ought to come to my wedding."

What an interesting and—yes, it was true—odd man. Wedding? Jonas had seemed so bouncy and, er, overly friendly, the captain had assumed ... Well, it wouldn't be the first time he was wrong about one of Thomas's friends.

"You're very kind. Perhaps I will, if my schedule allows."

"Lots of cake," Jonas wheedled. "You want some coffee?"

"Please."

Jonas bounced toward the kitchen, leaving the captain alone with the boy.

"You're looking well," he said after an uncomfortable silence.

"Thank you, sir."

"I was surprised to hear from you."

"No doubt, sir. Thank you," the boy said formally, "for coming so quickly."

"I was intrigued." Inwardly, the captain cursed himself for lying. Or at least not telling the whole truth. Yes, he had been intrigued. But he would have come no matter what the boy's request.

"Have you—have you had a chance to visit your mother's grave recently?"

"Yes," the boy said distantly.

"She, uh, always liked irises. Maybe sometime, we could—"

"Hi," a female voice said, and the captain glanced over the boy's shoulder.

Ah. The famous Fredrika Bimm. A doctor, like his boy. But not a *real* doctor—she was a scientist.

A damned good-looking one, too. The hair—such an unusual color! And green eyes—true green, not hazel. Tall and slender, neatly dressed in a button-down shirt and khaki shorts. Bare feet. There was something fresh and vital about her, something he couldn't help responding to, even though he was an old man.

He wished, again, that his poor wandering boy would settle down in one place and find someone to love, start a family. The boy deserved more family than he currently had: which was, of course, just the captain.

"Dr. Bimm," he said and tried not to wince when she shook his hand. *Holy hell, she's strong!* This was his first experience with a mermaid, though they'd certainly been all over the news lately. He'd been following the stories quite carefully. The military applications alone were so exciting, it was—

But then, that was why he was here, wasn't it?

"Captain Pearson. Thanks a lot for coming. We're just waiting on Prince Artur and then we can get started."

"The one who wanted the meeting is late?" he said, more sharply than he intended.

And then the lovely Dr. Bimm ripped him a new asshole.

"Yeah, well, *Captain*, we don't all run our empty, meaningless lives by a clock. Some of us, *Captain*, have families and loved ones to think about and those loved ones often throw wrenches into our schedules. Some of us, *Captain*, have entire kingdoms to worry about, as opposed to spending all of our time, hmm, I dunno, ignoring our only son."

The boy's eyes actually bulged. "Jesus, Fred!"

The captain laughed. And laughed. And finally had to sit down and hold his sides, because they ached so from such unaccustomed glee.

Thirty-eight

Fred eyed Thomas's father with thinly veiled suspicion. He looked like a typical military hard-ass, and from the moment she saw him she could guess how it had been between Captain Kick-ass and a son who had no interest in a military career.

Correction: a son who wrote romance novels and had no interest in a military career.

It made her ashamed for how much she took Moon and Sam for granted . . . for her occasional embarrassment at their hippie ways. Well, Moon would have lit herself on fire before trying to direct Fred's choice of career. Fred could have turned tricks and Moon never, ever would have cut off contact.

Funny. Funny to think that Moon and Sam had protested at Vietnam rallies in the sixties. Trying to end the war. Trying to get men like Pearson out of the jungle and back with his family.

Men like Pearson, who would have sneered at Moon's bell-bottoms and Sam's beard. Who would have called them fools for loving peace more than loving serving their country.

Yes, she could guess how it had been. It made her admire Thomas all the more for sticking to his choice, for denying his father's wishes and going his own way.

It was just another version of stage mothering, that's what it was. Or fathers pushing their sons into football so they could relive their long-gone glory days.

In a phrase, irritating beyond belief. She recalled a line from one of her favorite novels, *The Prince of Tides*. "Fuck the fathers. They should know better."

And wasn't that the truth.

Still. She could have chosen her words with a little more care. It was too bad she'd lost her temper a little.

Well. A lot.

And then he'd laughed. And laughed. And laughed!

So now Fred had no idea what to think, and she didn't like the feeling one bit. She didn't even know she was going to say it until it was out. And, like so many other things she said, once it was out, there was no taking it back.

There were so many things, she thought, staring at her now-present fiancé, you couldn't take back.

She couldn't deny it felt good to stick it to the old man—the thought of this guy not appreciating someone as wonderful as Thomas was fucking *infuriating*—but realized instantly that she'd antagonized their only source of military intelligence.

Amazingly, he hadn't minded.

Weird.

Really quite weird.

And then Artur had arrived, and she had to focus on the matter at hand.

The captain, to his credit, shook hands with Artur while looking him straight in the eye and *not* looking over-awed, as most people did when they met the imposing prince. They'd all had a seat at the big dining-room table.

Jonas had made coffee, put out platters of scrambled eggs and toast and jars of jelly, and had sat unobtrusively at the end of the table (most unusual!).

"Good sir, I am grateful you have come." Artur, who loved surface-dweller food, had a pile of scrambled eggs on his plate that resembled a yellow pyramid, three pieces of toast, and two cups of coffee. "My king has a problem and we need your assistance."

The captain, sitting ramrod straight in his chair (his spine didn't even touch the back!), nodded. He took a sip of his coffee and replied, "So my son implied. What's the trouble?"

Artur laid it out, quickly and precisely. The captain's eyebrows arched a few times (and how he looked like Thomas when he did that!) but he seemed to readily accept telepathy, missing Undersea Folk, the king's astonishing telepathic range, and how he and Artur discovered the problem. Fred was slightly amazed.

"I do not mean to impugn your honor by implying your government may be involved," Artur said carefully, "especially as Thomas has explained to me what a great warrior you were for your people."

Again with the eyebrow arch. Another glance at Thomas. And Thomas shrugged, something he was doing a lot with his father around. He was hardly saying anything at all—major-league unusual.

"But perhaps you may have some ideas about where we may look. Or perhaps you may strongly feel we are going in the wrong direction and can share that with us so we waste no more of your time. My people, and my father, would be grateful for any assistance you can give us, in whatever form that may be."

The captain smiled. It did amazing things to his craggy face: the years fell away. He had the same dimple Thomas did. His eyes, arctic blue, actually seemed to thaw. "Prince Artur, you will be an excellent king. I've rarely heard such potentially dangerous questions posed so diplomatically."

Artur inclined his head.

"You should see him juggle bowling pins," Jonas piped up from the end of the table, chomping on toast slathered with roughly an inch and a half of jelly.

Fred smirked in his direction.

"But I'm afraid our government would never, and has never, had anything to do with kidnapping, unlawfully detaining, or killing any of your people."

"Not the good people who brought us Fat Man and Little Boy," Fred said mockingly. "Or Agent Orange, the nuclear submarine, Japanese-American internment camps, the Thompson submachine gun, the long-range bomber, land-based ballistic missiles, or the B-52."

Thomas was actually covering his eyes. "Fred," he groaned.

Fred couldn't have stopped if someone had stuck a gun in her ear. "Of *course* the government isn't up to no good. Perish the thought!"

The captain quirked an eyebrow at her and the corner of his mouth turned up. "Why do you hate America, Dr. Bimm?" he asked pleasantly.

She threw her hands up in the air. "Oh, don't even start with that crap, Captain!"

"You look about the same age as my son. Hmmm. Let me guess: your parents were hippies? Antimilitary? Vietnam War protesters?"

"*Are* hippies," she corrected. "And yes. And yes."

"In other words, they were free to protest their

government's actions because the military secured that freedom for them."

"Children," Jonas said around a mouthful of eggs. "Play nice."

"Quite right, Jonas."

"Sorry," Fred muttered.

"Quite all right, Dr. Bimm. As I was saying, my government has not harmed or unlawfully detained any Undersea Folk. Not for military applications, not for border skirmishes, not for money, not for oil. Not for anything. I regret the loss of your people, but my government is blameless."

"I see." Artur was silent for a moment. "I am sorry to have wasted your time, Captain."

"It was no trouble. I was glad for the chance to see my boy again."

Thomas choked on his coffee. Fred had to pat him on the back when his face turned an alarming shade of purple.

"And, of course, I made a stop yesterday to visit some cronies at Sanibel Station—the naval base they have just down the road?"

"Sanibel Station?" Fred repeated, startled.

"There's a naval base on this teeny island?" Jonas asked.

Fred had no idea how to answer him. The navy often allowed marine biologists (or consulted with them) on various projects, and so Fred and Thomas, during their years of education and fieldwork, both had a working knowledge of most naval bases in the country.

And Thomas, of course, was the son of a naval officer. From the look on his face, he'd never heard of Sanibel Station, either.

"Well, perhaps I'm mistaken." The captain shrugged. "I'm getting old. My memory isn't what it used to be."

Thomas snorted into his coffee.

"Perhaps it's called something else. Or perhaps it's some*where* else. But regardless, it was nice to talk to some old friends. One of them—" The captain laughed, a freeing, joyful sound. "He's a sentimental idiot."

"That's . . ." Fred paused. "So sweet."

"Oh, he's always talking about how I carried him on my back through ninety yards of rice paddies to the chopper pickup. What crap! I keep telling him he's got the wrong guy. On paper, I was sixty miles away. That's what my orders said, anyway." He shook his head, still snorting laughter. "Like I said, he's an idiot. But it was nice to talk to him, all the same. Trading war stories. Finding out what former squad members have been up to. Silly old man stuff." Pause. "And it was very nice to see my son."

Thomas was staring at his father as if the man had sprouted a bathtub faucet from his forehead. For that matter, so was Fred.

The captain stood. Artur and Thomas stood. Fred and Jonas remained seated, Jonas because he was still chomping away, and Fred because her brain was working furiously to figure out just what the hell was going on.

"It was nice to meet you, Prince Artur."

"And you, Captain Pearson. I see now where Thomas gets his warrior spirit."

The captain shook his head. "No. He's his mother's son. For which I thank God every night." They shook hands, surface-dweller style.

Fred had to stand up and smack Jonas on the back. He really ought to stop eating until the captain left, she thought.

"Good to see you, son."

"You, too, sir." Thomas stuck out his hand.

And the captain put a fat file folder in it, with CLAS-SIFIED and EYES ONLY and PROJECT JAMMER stamped all over it in red.

Then he smiled.

Hugged his son (who was standing, frozen, and Fred feared he would drop the folder, or faint, or both).

Left.

Thirty-nine

"Uh," Jonas said. "What just happened?"

Thomas had dropped the folder on the table and started to sit. If Fred hadn't shoved the chair over, he would have landed splat on the floor. They were all staring at it.

Bulging with papers.

EYES ONLY.

CLASSIFIED.

"I can't believe he did that," Thomas murmured.

"I know!" Fred said, wide-eyed. "If it gets out that he gave us this, it'll be his ass!"

"I meant hugging me."

"Also extremely shocking. And just when I'd made up my mind that your dad was a dick."

"Fredrika," Artur reproved. "Do not speak so of such a warrior."

"Have you actually *met* me, Artur? For God's sake. So. Thomas, your dad made this happen." She pushed the folder over to him. "Why don't you do the honors?"

After a few seconds, he flipped open the folder. Passed chunks of paperwork around (the thing was two inches thick; it would have taken one person a week and a half to get through it).

They began to read.

Forty

🌊

King Mekkam came through the door. He didn't knock and get invited in. He didn't open it and walk through. He *burst* through the door and chunks of wood went flying everywhere.

Fred groaned, mentally kissing her security deposit good-bye.

"I came at once, my son."

"We noticed," Jonas said, big-eyed.

"What is so urgent? Are you all right?"

King Mekkam looked like a slightly older, grayer

version of Artur. They were even the same height. And, though the man was over a century old, he had the broad chest and shoulders of a lumberjack. His ruby-colored eyes glittered and he carried himself with an aloof dignity that proclaimed his royal blood far more efficiently than something so silly as a crown.

"We have had a fascinating visit from Thomas's sire," Artur replied.

"Fascinating isn't the word," Thomas muttered, rubbing his temples as if he were getting a headache. "Surreal. *Twilight Zone*–esque. In fact, it's possible that was an alien robot and not my father at all."

"You'd better have a seat, Mekkam," Fred said. "We've got lots of stuff to tell you."

The frown lines on his forehead disappeared and he smiled. "Fredrika!"

"You, uh, sound surprised to see me."

Mekkam shook his head, clasped her hands, then raised them to his mouth and kissed them. "I have not had an opportunity to tell you how very pleased I am that you are joining my family. I look forward to your mating ceremony and to many pups."

"Pups?" Jonas repeated. "Oh, God. This is too good. Pups?"

"They call being pregnant 'in pup,'" Fred explained, resisting the urge to strangle her friend. "So I'm guessing mer-babies are pups."

Jonas laughed harder.

"I hate you," Fred commented. "So much."

"But now, back to the matter at hand. What have you learned?"

They had reassembled the file and showed it to the king.

"What is Project Jammer?"

"It seems you have a few traitors in your midst, Mekkam," Thomas said heavily. "Some Undersea Folk apparently sought out a clandestine branch of the navy, a base called Sanibel Station that hardly anyone *in* the navy knows about. I imagine it's their version of Black Ops."

"Black Ops?" King Mekkam asked.

"It's usually a secret branch of the military, secret because there's often a question of ethics or legality involved," Thomas explained. "Our governments aren't supposed to send assassins or perform non-FDA-regulated experiments or think up new bioweapons or stuff like that, but of course they do. Everyone's government does. Black Ops exist so the government of whatever country is running the team has total deniability."

"Lots of sneaky stuff gets done that way," Fred added. "Among other things, research into unconventional warfare."

"Like telepathy," Jonas said.

Mekkam was silent. Then, "My . . . my people? Have done this? Gone to your military and . . . what, precisely?"

"Shown them what they can do, telepathically. Given them tissue samples. Submitted to experiments."

"But . . ." Mekkam looked so devastated, so horrified, Fred could hardly look at him. "Why?"

"So the navy could help them increase their telepathy," Thomas said, very quietly.

"You mean the people who disappeared . . . they did so . . . willingly? They allowed themselves to—" The king paused. Then a large fist slammed onto the table, which obligingly cracked. Everyone pushed their chairs back, but it only cracked down the middle; for the moment, it held together. "Then they are planning something. They are—" Shocked, he looked at Fred. "We were wrong. It isn't your father."

"No," Fred admitted, making no effort to hide her relief. "But it's probably some or all of the youngsters who sided with him during the coup. The ones who weren't banished, who apologized and made nice with everyone and pretended Farrem led them astray."

"And like a fool, I believed them!"

This time, the table broke under the blow. Fortunately, Jonas had cleared all the dishes while they were waiting for Mekkam to arrive.

"They probably meant it at the time," Jonas suggested, nervously eyeing the eight-foot table, now two four-foot tables. "So why wouldn't you have believed them? But after a while, they probably got to thinking . . . wondering if things could be different . . . and I'm betting you're not the kind of guy who spies on his people's thoughts just for funzies. So how could you have known?"

"No, no, I would never—" Mekkam sounded furious and bewildered, a frightening combination to watch. "I merely—I mean I don't *spy* on them like a filthy—"

"Mekkam, there's no way you could have seen this

coming," Fred said gently. "You got rid of the problem. The youngsters apologized. Nobody talked about Farrem anymore. That was that . . . for years and years."

"But why now? Why would they start disappearing from my mind in the last six months?"

"That's what we haven't been able to figure out," Thomas admitted. "Some of this report is pretty dense, and there are charts that Fred and I have to figure out. Some of it even appears to be in code. What we know so far is that some of your people have been working with the naval equivalent of a Black Ops team— probably a tit for tat."

"Pardon?"

"In return for giving the navy brain tissue samples, for letting doctors run tests on them, for basically being guinea pigs so the navy—that one, small, secret branch of the navy—can help them increase their telepathy, they've probably been running missions for the government."

"There's no way *any* government would have turned them down," Jonas added. "Fred warned you from the beginning that we, as a species, are incredibly nasty to anyone even slightly different. If the someone slightly different *volunteers* for, say, vivisection . . ."

"Now here come men and women who can breathe under water," Thomas said. "They're incredibly strong. They're incredibly long-lived and they age unbelievably well. You could send a man out with seventy years of combat experience, and he'd get carded if he tried to buy booze. Good stamina. Incredible swimmers—they're mermaids and mermen, for God's sake. The stuff of legend. And best of all, most wonderful of all, they're *telepaths*. And here comes a bunch of them willing to be experimented on if the navy will help them augment their innate abilities." Thomas paused to let this sink in. "Jonas is right. There's not a government on the planet who wouldn't have jumped at the chance."

"But why? Why do this?"

Fred paused. Surely the king *knew*. He was many things, none of them a fool. She put it down to shock. And she was sad for him. This was very likely a direct result of the Undersea Folk letting the world know they existed.

"Why try to make themselves stronger? Why disappear off your radar?" Thomas paused, then went on as gently as he could. "You've got another coup on your hands, Mekkam."

Forty-one

🦢

"How can we find out who they are?" Mekkam demanded.

Fred and Thomas exchanged glances. "Um," he began. "That's a little tricky. Other than storming a secret naval base on Sanibel Island, I don't have a clue. And with all respect, Mekkam, I don't think you want to go to war with the United States Navy. Which means the United States." He paused. "We fight dirty. We fight to win."

"Fat Man and Little Boy," Fred muttered. She didn't

dare mention Hiroshima . . . Mekkam was having a bad enough day.

"I cannot sit back and wait to be attacked. If it were only my life, I would not mind. But I must think of my son—of our future queen—and my people."

"Ack!" Fred choked. "Please, *please* don't factor me into any of this. Artur and the Undersea Folk, absolutely. But I can take care of myself. Please don't worry about me. You've got enough problems."

"Do not underestimate your father's people, Fredrika. News of your betrothal has spread from mind to mind at the speed of thought. You would make an excellent target."

"Big deal, she's been hearing that since the third grade," Jonas scoffed. "Usually from me."

"Don't forget, Mekkam, I have zero trouble hanging out on land indefinitely. Any UF who comes after me is risking major dehydration. I'll be safe as long as I stay out of the water."

"I recommend moving to the Sahara," Thomas said. "Today."

"I'll help you pack," Jonas offered.

"I'll help you help her pack," Thomas added.

"Everyone calm down. And nobody's touching my things. Listen, we've agreed storming the naval base is baaaaad. Right?"

Nods all around. Except for Mekkam. Mekkam's gaze was fixed on her. She wondered when he was planning to blink.

"Well. These guys, whoever they are, they've disappeared off Mekkam's radar, right? Maybe *specifically* his radar. Maybe they've been augmented, or whatever, strictly for the purpose of hiding from Mekkam's telepathy, maybe the whole royal family's telepathy."

"Yes, yes, my Rika. We know this."

"We've surmised it," Thomas corrected. "We don't *know* shit."

"Well. Who's the most powerful telepath after the royal family?"

Dead silence.

"Who would these guys never *dream* of being a threat because he's been banished for decades?"

Finally, from Artur, "He will never help us. We made his name unspeakable. We banished him to a friendless life, to die alone. We—"

"Yeah, yeah, I know all about it. But I've been talking

with him—you remember, he's sleeping here at night—and he's fine with it. Well. Not *fine*. But he's older now, you know, and he's sorry. He's had years and years to think about his mistakes. And in the interim he's made an entirely new life for himself. Believe me, Artur, my father would *leap* at the chance to help you guys."

"Leap?" Mekkam said doubtfully.

"Like a frog on cocaine," Fred confirmed. "But if you want his help, we need to ask him *now*. He's leaving any day. He's afraid that if he sticks around it'll cause trouble for me."

"That is . . . thoughtful," Artur admitted. "I will say, the Farrem I knew was not remotely thoughtful."

"You want to talk to him?"

"Yes, Fredrika. I do."

"Then you can do it in about an hour." Fred glanced around at the group. "He told me last night he was seeing to some business this morning; he was headed for a FedEx drop-off. Payroll or some such crap; I wasn't paying much attention. But we're supposed to have lunch today." She glanced at the clock on the far wall. "In sixty minutes."

Thomas stood. "I think we've got some hamburger left in the fridge. I can fire up the grill."

"I shall catch some fish," Artur said, also standing. "I detest sitting around waiting. Join me, Rika?"

"Ah, no, thanks, Artur." On the off chance her father showed up early, she wanted to make sure she was here. Who knew how the meeting would go without her? It could end up a cluster fuck. Or worse: more of the furniture could get broken.

Forty-two

§

Fifty-five minutes later, her father walked through the large hole that was once her front door. "Fredrika, are you well? What in the king's name happened here? Did you—"

He saw the group waiting for him and stopped short.

The king cleared his throat. "Greetings, Farrem."

Farrem couldn't have looked more amazed if the king had kissed him on the mouth. "G-greetings, my king. Prince Artur. Thomas. Jonas. Fredrika." He paused and took another step into the house. "May I ask what is going on? Has someone been hurt? Fredrika? Is your lady mother all right?"

"My lady mother and Sam are at SeaWorld for the day, thank God. We need your help, Farrem. Do you have some time? Can you talk to us for a little bit?"

"Certainly." He eyed the broken table and sat down in an empty dining-room chair without comment.

As they explained the situation and showed him bits from the classified file, Farrem's eyes got wider and wider.

"But this is my fault!" he cried, shoving the file away from him as if it were hot. "They *must* be some of my old followers. And they never would have— would have let surface dwellers *do* things to them if I hadn't—if I—" He looked up at Mekkam, stricken. "My king, I am so very sorry. Count on me. I will do whatever you require to make amends."

Mekkam, who had been sitting stiffly (as stiffly as Artur . . . both of them looked as flexible as mannequins), relaxed slightly. "I thank you, Farrem. Our people will be most grateful for your help. But . . ." He seemed to struggle with the words, then coughed them up. "But you are not responsible for what youngsters decided to do once they attained a few years. Our society has ever been about free will."

"Hey, so is ours," Jonas whined.

"You are kind, my king. But my debt is great. I am grateful for the chance to pay it off." Her father smiled grimly. "Including the interest."

Forty-three

"What in the name of the king happened to your door?"

"Funny how people keep using *that* phrase," Jonas sighed.

Tennian and Wennd were standing in the hole where the door used to be, and Fred figured it was about time to find a gallon of Off! and pour it over her head.

Tennian shook her head as if trying to come back to herself. "Forgive me, my king, the door is irrelevant."

"Says the woman who didn't have to cough up a four-figure security deposit," Fred grumped.

"You called and I have come."

"Thank you, Tennian."

"Four figures," Fred reminded them. "Down the drain."

"Oh, shut up and dig into your trust fund," Jonas hissed. "Priorities, dammit!"

"Besides the prince and me, you are the only member of the royal family within three thousand miles. We need your courage today of all days. And I needed to make sure you were safe." The king turned to the beautiful violet-haired mermaid. "Wennd, this is none of yours, young one," Mekkam said gently. "I wish for you to return to the Indian Ocean as quickly as you can."

"I—I was with her when you called, my king."

Fred couldn't help looking at the beautiful woman, but it wasn't the hair or the eyes that had her attention. There was something about Wennd that was bugging her, and damned if she could put her finger on it.

"I want to help," Wennd whispered. "Please let me help. Don't send me away if my people are in danger."

Artur smiled at her. "Very well, Wennd. I should hate to reward such loyalty with dismissal."

What was it about her? Fred wondered if it was something so simple as concern. Wennd was so timid and gentle, Fred wasn't crazy about the thought of her getting hurt. She really had no business here. Things could get nasty.

She wished the king had made her leave.

Tennian, meanwhile, had marched up to Farrem. "It appears you are redeeming yourself," she managed through clenched teeth, hands on hips, staring up into his face. "I am grateful, on behalf of my family, for your assistance. I . . . regret my rudeness earlier."

Farrem laughed, but it wasn't mean. It was a cheery laugh and Fred grinned, despite the seriousness of the situation. "No, Tennian, you do not. But it is kind of you to swallow your ire for the sake of your king."

"Mmph." As a comeback, Fred thought, it wasn't much, but at least Tennian wasn't tackling her father or throwing him through the kitchen window. Progress! "What are we doing?"

"Farrem has kindly agreed to try to locate those who have hidden themselves from me," Mekkam explained.

"If he does, and if he can pinpoint their locations, we will form teams and go after them."

"How many of us are in these waters?" Farrem asked.

"Seven hundred sixty-four, not counting the ones I can no longer 'see.'"

Jonas whistled, but Artur shook his head. "A mere fraction. If what we fear is true, and we face war against artificially augmented traitors . . ."

The king nodded grimly. "I will mobilize all the Folk in the area and we will hunt them down."

Fred wondered what that meant. She knew that in general, Undersea Folk abhorred killing one another. It was almost unthinkable.

"One coup in a lifetime is quite enough," Mekkam continued grimly. "I would this one were thwarted before it truly began."

Fred leaned over and whispered in Farrem's ear, "Told you they'd give you another chance if you gave them one. Thirty years was long enough."

"You did tell me," he admitted, *not* whispering, "but I put it down to the naïveté of extreme youth."

"Well, thanks a heap, *Dad.*"

"Farrem, if you please," Mekkam asked, except

everyone in the room knew it was a royal command. "Please try to locate the lost ones."

Lost ones, Fred thought. That was an awfully generous way to put it.

Farrem nodded and sat back down in the dining-room chair. He leaned forward, resting his elbows on his knees, and closed his eyes.

The room felt . . . Fred didn't know exactly how to describe it . . . it felt *thick*. Charged, even, the way it felt before a kick-ass thunderstorm. And if she could sense that, what must Tennian and Wennd and Artur and Mekkam be feeling?

Cripes, Farrem calling . . . searching . . . it must be like a megaphone in their heads!

Farrem's shoulders started to tremble. His face was hidden in his hands as he concentrated. In seconds he was shaking all over.

Suddenly, shockingly, Wennd's odd, goose-like laugh sounded through the room, making them all jump. And she was just—she was just standing there, holding her stomach and laughing.

And Farrem looked up.

He was laughing, too.

Forty-four

"You really thought I was going to help you. Didn't you, Mekkam?"

Fred clutched the arm of her chair so hard, she felt it splinter beneath her fingers. Too late, she had it. The thing that was bugging her.

"Dammit!" She was staring at the hee-hawing Wennd. "You live in the Indian Ocean. And my father has a house in Perth. Which is on the Indian Ocean." Aarrgghh! She was a fucking marine biologist, she knew her geography, which countries and cities bordered which oceans. They had both dumped a large clue in her lap, and she hadn't suspected a thing.

Moron!

"Nice," Thomas said, his mouth twisting in distaste. "You sent your girlfriend to spy on us."

"Of course I did."

"That 'scared of surface dweller' thing," Jonas said. "Nice act."

"Do not speak to me," Wennd said by way of reply.

Artur was on his feet. "You will address my father as 'my king' or 'Your Majesty.' "

"Actually, that's how you'll address me. If you were going to live through this. Which you won't. Sit down."

Slowly, looking astonished, Artur did so.

"Why do I feel like I came into the middle of the movie?" Jonas asked.

"Because you're a worm," her father replied. He wasn't even mean about it. Perfectly casual, the way Fred would have said, "because you have blue eyes."

"You won't get away with this, Farrem. You didn't before," Fred said. "Also, not to be a nag or anything, but this really isn't the way to win back the royal family's trust."

"Do not speak to me, you stupid girl. I've known anemones that had more intelligence."

"That seems uncalled for," Jonas said.

"I know. I think he needs a nap. He's getting grumpy and he was up late last night, poor tyrannical baby."

"Be *quiet*! To think, a child of mine who can't read, who can't speak our language, much less possess the rudimentary telepathy an *infant* is born with! I cannot believe your mother let you live."

"Yeah, well, she's full of flaws like that."

"I've told Moon and told her," Jonas said, "she just has to step up the baby-killing. But she never listens."

"And by the way, *Dad*—"

"I ordered you not to speak to me."

"—there's more of us in this house than you. Why, exactly, are we not going to rip your treacherous heads off?"

He smirked. "I confess to shock; I thought the prince or the king might ask that. Not you. I wasn't working this morning, stupid. Well, I was, but not the way you think. I stopped by Sanibel Station—very helpful, some of those surface worms—and made sure that Captain Pearson worm was going to leave with the file."

"What?" Thomas asked, his voice dangerously low. "You got my dad involved in this?"

"Not at all. It was just a delicious coincidence that he was going to stop by to try to get information for you. I knew Mekkam would eventually notice something was wrong, and I knew my idiot daughter would have a worm friend somewhere that could help her."

"Did he just call *moi* a worm friend?" Jonas asked.

"No," Thomas said. *"Moi."*

Looking annoyed that the three of them weren't more terrified, Farrem continued, "I made sure one of his worm friends had access to it."

"So we're supposed to believe you *wanted* us to have your super-secret file?" Jonas asked skeptically.

Fred, meanwhile, was wondering why Tennian, Artur, and Mekkam weren't moving or speaking.

A megaphone in their heads. That's why.

"Of course I did! Because I knew even if I *literally* handed you the plan, you'd be too dim to comprehend it. And I knew that what little you could figure out would inspire the stupid girl to suggest they ask for my help."

"I have to admit," Fred said, "that wasn't one of my brightest ideas."

243

"Like the time you tried to eat two packages of Mint Milanos with Baileys chasers," Jonas agreed.

Farrem hissed through his teeth, appeared to recover his temper, then turned to Fred. "I so enjoyed our little talk by the pool, girl. I knew you were dim, but that conversation confirmed it, even before I realized you were mind blind. I certainly dropped enough hints."

And so he had, Fred realized, cursing herself. When he called her stupid, he wasn't so far off.

Perth.

So you did sort of get your own kingdom, after all.

Just because your father, and grandfather, and great-grandfather had been king, that didn't mean that you should be king.

My gift and my curse.

Your mother's blood is strong in you.

I naturally assumed one of my blood . . . You are your mother's daughter.

Awww. She had disappointed her papa. Oh, the shame of it!

She couldn't have been more thrilled. It was hard not to chortle.

Like a typical James Bond villain, her doorknob dad

244

was still bragging about his clever plan. "So after thirty years, I was again face-to-face with my enemies. And they were kind enough to bring the royal cousin, too!"

Wennd smirked. "She was planning to swim down to La Habana today. But I kept her in the area." Fred noticed that her normal voice was not a whisper. In fact, it was rather nasal and grating, like Madison when she had a head cold and had eaten too many Mentos.

"Too bad," Fred said.

"What?" Wennd asked, seeming surprised that Fred was speaking to her.

"You're not beautiful anymore," she said simply, and Jonas and Thomas nodded in agreement.

"Your sire told you not to speak."

"Yeah, well, *Dad* hasn't been paying much attention this past week if he thinks that'll shut me up. What's the matter, Farrem? Is something not going according to plan?" Slowly, Fred stood.

Wennd actually took a step backward. "You said they wouldn't be able to move, Farrem. You promised you could control—"

"Quiet," he snapped.

"Tough luck about your daughter being the UF

equivalent of retarded. Mind blind, isn't that the phrase? Are you trying to telepathically control me right now, Pop? Because I couldn't help but notice I can think and talk and move without any trouble at all. So I guess I'll be kicking your ass starting right about now."

"Even now," Farrem said, "even now my people are starting to take over. They're subduing any Undersea Folk they can find. None of them will be able to move or speak until I say so. It is through me that my people can control yours, Mekkam! My stupid daughter and her idiot worm friends couldn't break the codes or decipher the charts."

"Well, of course not. The thing was a thousand pages long. They only had it for a couple of hours," Jonas said reasonably. "Way to play fair, ya big pussy."

It really wasn't the time or place, but Fred had to hide a smile. It was her and Jonas and Thomas against the super strong, super quick, super psychotic nutbag (and his super strong and quick henchwoman/girlfriend) who had boned her mother on a Cape Cod beach. And Jonas and Thomas were acting like it was lunch at McDonald's. Nothing extraordinary going on here, no way, nuh-uh.

"If they'd had the sense to understand what I *handed*

them," Farrem ground out, "they would have understood my people weren't getting enhanced, they were
swimming about the world doing—isn't this a funny
phrase?—wet work."

"What's—" Jonas began.

"Assassinations," Thomas said.

"Of course that's what it means." Jonas sighed.
"And here I thought they were designing water parks."

"Will you *stop talking*?" Farrem shrieked. They
were clearly ruining his gloating supervillain moment
by not being terrified. "I paid for my enhancement . . .
for the drugs, and the treatments, the *years* of biopsies
and operations and experiment after experiment—I
paid Sanibel Station with my people. They did the
work and I got enhanced. Enhanced enough to hide
them from *you*, Mekkam, you pious whale. Enhanced
so that you will not move or speak unless *I* wish it."

"Truly inspiring leadership," Thomas commented.
"Making the team do the dirty work while you lie
around on a Valium drip getting experimented on."

Jonas laughed.

Farrem glared dead into Fred's eyes. "I will kill
them if you don't shut them up."

"Like you wouldn't kill them anyway?"

"I'd kill us anyway," Jonas said. "Thomas?"

He nodded. "Oh, yeah. I'd have quit babbling ten minutes ago and killed us, to be honest."

"In fact," Jonas added, "if you're going to keep talking, *would* you please kill us? Right now?"

"Your worm friends think they're funny. Shut them up if you value them in any way."

Fred shrugged. "Believe me, I've been trying for years. But kill them if you can. Problem is, you fucked up, Farrem. Big-time."

"You really are enormously stupid," he marveled. "Even now, you cannot comprehend it is over. I am king. Very soon Mekkam and Artur will be dead. Don't you understand? I can *make* them kill themselves! I won't even have to lift a finger! And you! I can't have you *breeding*."

"Well, I wasn't going to do it right this minute."

"You're disgusting and your deficiencies will die with you."

She was fairly certain no one had ever looked at her with such loathing—not even that waiter at the Hancock Tower Legal Sea Foods.

"You're a freak, a genetic joke. You're not a worm and you're not one of my people. You can't be allowed to breathe for another minute."

"Yeah, yeah, and you're going to ground me and take away my car keys. Can you think of the part of that story you *shouldn't* have told me?" she asked sweetly. She forced her fingers to loosen on the armrests.

She had to keep him on land. Had to. If they went in the water, he'd have the upper hand and it would be all over. And not just for her. She could never take on a full-blooded UF in the water. Certainly not a psychotic one.

And she had to get him out of the house, keep him away from Jonas and Thomas. No hostage-taking today, thank you.

She prayed Dr. Barb wouldn't be back anytime soon, but kept her tone light and teasing.

"Daddy-o? Can you?"

Jonas was waving a hand in the air. "I know, I know! Pick me!"

"Yeah, you should pick him." Thomas yawned. "He always gets picked last."

"Shut *up*!" Farrem said.

"But it's true," Jonas said earnestly. "I do always get picked last."

"The thing you shouldn't have told me is the part about how you're the enhanced one. Not your followers."

Then Thomas produced his switchblade—from where, Fred had no idea. One minute his hand was empty, the next there was a snick of sound and Thomas was holding a knife, turning, throwing it.

Right into Wennd's throat.

Forty-five

🌊

Farrem shrieked and clutched his head. He was powerful enough so that his grip on Artur's and Mekkam's and Tennian's minds did not lessen, but hearing Wennd's death screams in his head couldn't have been too comfortable.

Fred dove across the table at him, her momentum carrying them both through the glass patio door. The sound was a thousand teacups breaking at once.

Good. Good. Get the fight away from Thomas and

Jonas. And keep Farrem out of the water. If he ever got into his tail form, the fight was over.

And so was everything else.

His fist looped toward her face but she ducked, and then they were rolling across her lawn, Farrem choking and gagging on grass. When they stopped, Fred was on top and the pool was less than seven feet away.

"Your girlfriend's having a real bad day, did you notice?" she asked, then brought her head down and broke her father's nose with a muffled crunch. It hurt her forehead, but not as much as it hurt him, and that was just fine.

He howled and punched out at her, but he was distracted by the blood running down his throat and, she imagined, Wennd's dying screams running through his big, stupid brain. She tried to follow up but he managed to buck her off. He scuttled like a crab, clawing through the grass in an attempt to get to the pool. She leapt forward and caught a handful of his thick green hair, so like hers.

She *hated* her hair. She yanked. Hard. Farrem yowled. A lot.

She dragged him away from the pool. Yep, he was

stronger than she was, no doubt. Probably smarter, too, she'd give him that—it was a good plan. Everything had come about the way he predicted it would. It would have worked, if not for the Freak That Was Fred.

But she'd spent her life hiding her mermaid nature, blending with surface dwellers. She'd been raised by hippies, for God's sake. She was a helluva lot more comfortable on land than he was. Banished or not, big houses or not, he still couldn't stay out of the water for very long. And the longer he was out, the weaker he got.

She could stay out of it for weeks, and had.

She yanked harder, a thought

(am I actually enjoying this?)

there and gone before she could catch it. His hair (and some of his scalp) came off in her hand and then he was again getting to his feet, this time heading for the dock.

Too slow. Again. She leapt for him, landing on his back like dear old Dad was giving dumb Daughter a piggyback ride. She grabbed his chin in both hands. And wrenched to the left, hard.

The crack was undramatic, the sound a walnut makes

when it's crushed in the nutcracker. But Farrem dropped like a rock.

A big, green-haired, psychotic, dead rock.

She didn't even have time to comprehend she had won—it had been so *fast*! He'd only revealed himself, what? Fifteen minutes ago? But there was no time to understand what had happened because someone from behind yanked her off his body.

She rolled, trying to scramble to her feet to face the new threat

(oh, man, which henchmen is this now?)

only to see Thomas standing over her father's corpse. He brought a foot down on Farrem's rib cage, hard.

"You were dead the minute you called her stupid, motherfucker! When you said her mother should have drowned her! Your girlfriend's *dead*! You're *dead*! You can't touch her, *ever*! Get up, you piece of shit! Get up so I can feed you your balls!" Another crunch as the left ribs caved in.

"Thomas!" She grabbed him from behind, dodged (barely) the elbow he brought back, and carefully pulled him away from the corpse. "He's dead, Thomas. He's already dead. It's pointless. The prick can't feel a thing. Unfortunately," she added.

"Put me down, please, Fred," he said, perfectly calmly.

She did.

He turned, grabbed her face with both hands, and kissed her so hard she felt it in her knees.

Which, of course, was the moment Artur and Mekkam and Tennian came staggering out the broken patio door.

Thomas pointed to Artur. "And you can't have her, either."

"Holy shit!" Jonas said, peeking around Tennian. "What'd we miss?" Then, "I'm not cleaning any of this up."

Forty-six

They were all sprawled in various spots in the living room.

"Thank God," Jonas moaned, "thank God Barb was out shopping for a wedding dress."

"Thank God he made the classic Bond villain mistake," Thomas said.

Fred, who was sprawled almost prone, sat up. "That's exactly what I thought!"

"I cannot believe," Mekkam was muttering, "that Wennd fooled me."

"And me," Tennian added. She and Artur and Mekkam were moving very gingerly and holding their heads; it was clear they had crushing headaches. "I'm sorry Thomas killed her; I so wanted that pleasure for myself."

"And Thomas! Way to stud up, man! You threw that knife, what? Eight feet? *Zam*, right into her neck." Jonas shook his head. "How many of those things do you have? And where do you keep them?

"Enough." Thomas looked grim. "We got lucky. I was aiming for her eye."

"But what was she doing here? Farrem said himself that he was the enhanced one, that he was lending his power to his followers."

"Isn't it obvious?" Jonas asked. Fred scowled, because it wasn't. "He had her here just in case Fred didn't warm up to him. He had no guarantee she'd be friendly—shit, he was probably amazed when she offered him a guest room."

"Not one of your brighter moves," Thomas needled.

"Tell me. And that reminds me. Call the fumigator."

"So she was his 'just in case.' And he made sure the captain had the file," Jonas added, clearly warming to his subject (he'd been a huge *Encyclopedia Brown* fan in elementary school), "because it was the one thing that would make Artur yell for his dad. Once Mekkam got here, it was inevitable that Fred would suggest what she did. Then Farrem had all the royals—the ones in this area, anyway—in one spot. If Fred had been vulnerable to his giant evil brain blasting power, it would have worked perfectly."

"Fortunately," Fred said cheerfully, "I'm defective."

"So are all his followers," Mekkam said, gingerly holding his head. "They died when he died. I felt it. He could no longer hide them from me, and without his protection, they were helpless."

"But he *knew* Fred was—what was it? Mind blind? Why'd he still try it?"

"Because he was sure he and Wennd were more than a match for two worms and a freak," Fred said sourly. "Classic Bond villain mistake number two."

"Fredrika."

"At least it's over," she said.

"Fredrika."

"What?" And then she realized. It was Artur, and he

wasn't calling her my Rika, or Little Rika, or any term of endearment.

"Will you step outside with me?" he asked quietly and, with a glance at Thomas, she rose and followed him through the hole that used to be her front door.

They stood in the front yard (Farrem's corpse was still on the back lawn), Artur with his arms crossed over his chest, Fred fidgeting.

"Thomas seemed quite sincere about his intentions toward you when he finished with your father's body," he said, mildly enough.

"Uh, yeah."

"What are your thoughts on that?"

"That I'm a coward."

He smiled. "Hardly."

"I'm not in love with you, Artur, but I like you an awful lot. I think you're awesome. But I can't be your queen." *Among other things, I can't do that to the Undersea Folk gene pool.*

And Thomas wants me. He wants me!

"Part of the reason I said yes was because I planned to spend the rest of my life hiding in the Black Sea.

Running away from the messiness of hybrid life. It's a rotten way to start a marriage, never mind a family. It would have been a shitty thing to do to you."

"You were wrong. In your interview, you were wrong."

That was so unexpected, she couldn't immediately process it. "What?"

He took her hands in his, looking down into her eyes. "When you save an Undersea Folk—at least, when you save this one—you do get a wish. I release you from your word. You are no longer she-who-will-be-my-mate."

She wrenched her hands away and flung her arms around his neck. "Thank you, Artur. Thank you, thank you. I'll always be your friend. And the next time a megalomaniac tries to kill the royal family, you better come get me!"

He kissed the top of her head and hugged her back. "Agreed, Fredrika."

And if he had seemed the smallest bit relieved, she was going to pretend she hadn't noticed. She didn't know if he had fallen out of love with her, or if he had realized that the chase was more fun than the engagement, and she didn't care.

They would always be friends. He was, after all, her prince.

Forty-seven

It seemed like they were cleaning up the mess (it was considered strictly an Undersea Folk matter and, thank God, the nearest neighbor was too far away to have heard anything amiss) for hours.

Mekkam ate six Advil and took charge. Little by little, the bodies were taken away, the damage to her home was repaired (or at least boarded up), and by the time she had the house to herself (and her roommates), Fred was exhausted.

And slightly amazed. Because the Undersea Folk treated her like royalty. Ironic, given that she wasn't ever going to be royalty.

They were anxious about the repairs to her rental—did they meet with her approval? Would she prefer another table? Was it all right if they couldn't replace the patio glass until tomorrow? Because if not, they would see to it that—

The fight, it seemed, had been seen in the mind of all the Undersea Folk in the area. Farrem had been projecting everything, a sadistic touch to ensure their cooperation, to make sure they knew who was in charge. Knew who had taken over. Knew who was going to kill the king and prince.

Knew who was going to get his neck broken by a half-breed mind blind marine biologist with split ends.

"It's almost a shame you're not engaged to Artur anymore," Jonas whispered to her, watching their deference in awe. "Also, I'm not speaking to you because I really, really wanted to plan a royal wedding."

"Go soak your head," she whispered back.

Amazing! All you had to do to earn their admiration was break your father's neck on your back lawn.

"What a week," she groaned, stumbling into her room. It was two thirty in the morning and she needed a shower in the worst way.

"Say it twice," Thomas said. She heard the bedroom door close and realized with a start this was the first moment they'd had alone all day.

"Sit," he ordered, and, sighing, she obeyed. He *would* go into M.D. mode, of course, even though she was perfectly fine except for a few cuts (from the patio glass) and bruises (from the fight). But she was a fast healer, and he didn't need to poke or prod.

"Thomas, really, I'm—"

"I love you," he said, bending so he could look her in the eyes. She could feel her own eyes widening. "I've always loved you. And I was stupid about it. I thought Artur was the best thing for you and I didn't fight for you and I damned near made the worst mistake of my life. I'm scared shitless you'll get hurt. I'm scared shitless I'll have to hurt you again to fix you—like in Boston.

"But I'm even more scared at the prospect of a life without you. So we're getting married. Right away."

"Are you asking me?" she asked, feeling the bubble of joy spread from her heart all the way into her throat. It was actually hard to talk, she was so happy. "Or telling me?"

"Shut up and kiss me," he said, smiling, and she did. In seconds they were rolling around on her bed, groping and kissing and moaning and clutching.

"Wait, wait," she gasped. "I'm gross. I've still got Farrem's blood under my nails."

"I could use a shower, too." For a moment he looked grim, and she realized the healer was wrestling with the avenging lover. "It's not every day I throw a knife into a woman's neck."

"A woman who helped Farrem plot the deaths of hundreds, at the very least. Or did you think he was going to pick some other ridiculously beautiful woman to be his queen?"

"True enough. Come on." He stood and held out a hand. She took it and he pulled her to her feet. "I'll wash your back."

"That's nice. I'll wash your front."

And so they did, and when they were clean they stayed under the pounding spray, kissing until their lips were numb, soaping breasts and balls and buttocks, running slick hands all over slick flesh, gliding, sliding, and Fred was actually having trouble determining where one of them stopped and the other began.

And then, ah, God, he was lifting her, and entering her, and she was arching her back and meeting his thrusts, her fingers were digging into the heavy muscles of his shoulders, and at the height of her orgasm he kissed her on the side of her throat and she thought, *Home, home, I've never really felt like I belonged anywhere but right this minute I'm home, oh, thank you, God, I'm home at last.*

Epilogue

"This dress itches."

"Quit bitching, Fred."

"And this bouquet has made me sneeze twice."

"I mean it, Fred."

"And I'm hot. It's fucking ninety degrees out here and I'm in a floor-length dress!"

"So is Barb, so shut your hole."

"When is this thing going to *start* already?"

"It has started. You'd just rather be off somewhere banging Thomas."

"As a matter of fact, I would."

"Disgusting," Jonas said smugly, adjusting his bow tie. "You two are like monkeys. *Loud* monkeys."

"Look who's talking! How many scenes of debauchery have I walked in on? At least we've got the decency to keep to our bedroom." *And our shower. And the hot tub. And the pool when everyone's asleep. And—*

"I get that you haven't had sex in, what? Eight years?"

"Jonas," she warned grimly.

"But you two are going to hurt each other if you keep trying to make up for lost time."

"Jonas, I'm five seconds away from hanging you by your cummerbund. I'll get the electric chair, of course, but it's a small price to pay."

"Wait!" Jonas cocked his head as the tempo of the music changed. "That's your cue. Go, go!"

"Why are you even back here?" she demanded. "The bridesmaids are supposed to be back here." The other two had already gone, and hallelujah.

"To make sure you don't head for the hills." He gave her a rude shove in the middle of her back. "Now get going! I'll duck around the side and pop out in front."

"Great. It's not a wedding, it's a fucked-up magic show."

"Sparkle, Fred, sparkle!" Then, before she could pummel him, he had darted away.

She stomped down the aisle, recognizing several guests: Artur, Tennian, Mekkam. Her mother and Sam. Colleagues from the New England Aquarium, including (*oh, God*) Madison.

The captain, in full dress uniform, sitting beside Thomas. They both smiled at her as she passed them and Fred marveled at the change in her fiancé's father. The man had seriously mellowed after his wife's death. He'd certainly been nice enough to *her*, even going so far as to give Thomas his late mother's wedding and engagement rings to present to Fred. Fred had been proud to accept the engagement ring and, in another month, would be wearing the wedding ring as well.

Even though she'd been wearing it for over a month, she couldn't help being distracted by it now and again. It was a nice piece of jewelry, a platinum band with a half-carat diamond setting, but that's not why she caught herself staring at it during inopportune moments.

She loved what it represented, that was all. Almost as much as she loved the man who had given it to her.

She tipped him a wink, and prayed Jonas wouldn't notice she had refused to wear the silver heels he'd picked out for her.

Barefoot, she padded up the aisle to take her place beside Dr. Barb, who was looking dazzling in a cream-colored dress Jonas had selected. Dr. Barb looked exhilarated and intimidated and thrilled, all at once.

As the music reached its crescendo, she leaned in and whispered to the bride, "By the way, I'm withdrawing my resignation."

"What resignation?" the bride whispered back. "And you'd better not be late next Monday."

Real romantic, that's what it was.

Fred buried her face in her bouquet and snorted laughter into the white roses.

Turn the page for a special preview of
MaryJanice Davidson's new novel

Undead and Unwelcome

Coming soon from Berkley Sensation!

"So, if I'm reading this correctly, you're a vampire now. Not a secretary."

"Administrative assistant," I corrected automatically. I mean, jeez! I knew Cooper was old and creaky, but what century does he think this is?

"The important thing that's emphasized here," Cooper went on patiently, "is the bit about the vampires."

"Well, yeah."

"And how you're the queen of them."

"I guess some people would consider that an important point."

"It's bulleted. Also, the date of your death is bulleted, along with how you don't have to pee anymore."

"Give me that thing." I snatched the memo away from Cooper so quickly, he didn't see my hand move until his wrinkly fingers were clutching air. This startled him into a gasp, which we then both pretended I hadn't heard. That, I was learning, was vampire etiquette. Or, that is, vampire etiquette when dealing with humans. There should be a class, you know. Vampire Etiquette When Dealing with Humans 101. In another fifty years, I could teach the stupid thing.

I scanned the memo, my eyes bulging so much they felt like they were trying to leap from my skull. My God! Cooper hadn't been kidding. Jessica *had* sent him a memo about me. Two pages!

To: Samuel Cooper. From: The Boss. Re: Betsy, Vampirism, and Cargo.

Cargo?

And the part about me being the vampire queen *was* bulleted.

"I can't believe she sent you a memo."

"She always does. To keep me in the loop, don't you know. Seems that one's a little late, though," he muttered.

" 'Creepy speed and unnaturally grotesque super strength'?" Aghast, I kept reading as other blechy phrases leaped out at me. " 'Still obsessed with shoes but married rich and can now actually afford the stupid things'? Oh, my God! That scrawny traitor, I'm going to—agh! 'Immortality hasn't given her any interest in any subject not directly involving her life.' Why, that— Okay, I can't really argue with that last one, but she didn't have to highlight it. Look! It's *highlighted*."

"So I'm to fly you to Cape Cod," Cooper continued relentlessly, a dog with a bone. My God, the dumb stuff this guy was obsessing about . . . "So you can meet with the king of the werewolves and to make sure he doesn't sic his pack on you."

"I think it's pronounced Pack."

Cooper heard the capital P (I know how it sounds, but you really could hear it if you pronounced it the right way) and nodded. "Right. This Pack, they're pretty ticked? Because of that little gal Antonia?"

I nibbled on the inside of my lip, distressed, as always, by any mention of Antonia. It had only been three days, so the sting was still fresh. Sting! More like a lateral slice through the liver.

See, poor Antonia was making the trip with us. Via the cargo area, I was sorry to say. In a plain wooden coffin, the lethal bullet holes all over her body still not covered by an undertaker. My husband, Sinclair, and I had no idea what werewolf funeral customs entailed, so we'd given orders that her body simply be placed in a coffin and loaded onto Jessica's private plane.

We didn't even wash her face. Her beautiful, dear face.

But that was nothing compared to what we did with Garrett's body.

"Look, Cooper, the important thing is now you know what you're getting into. So if you can't fly us out there, or if you think you—"

"Bite your tongue, miss. Or missus, I suppose. I've been flying for Jessica Wilson since she was seven years old, don't you know, and we've had hair days and we've had *hairy days*. I've seen and heard things— Never mind, that's private family business."

"Oh, come on, Jessica and I are best friends. There's no way you know stuff that I don't—"

Cooper ruthlessly interrupted my shameless wheedling for gossip. "*This* doesn't scare me." He nodded at the memo, inadvertently crumpled in my fist. "But I surely wish Miss Jessica had told me earlier."

He meant, but wouldn't say, "Like, how about before I flew you and the vampire king to New York City for your honeymoon, dumbass?" Or maybe I would say that but he would think it. Anyway, the good news was that Cooper was neither (a) freaked out, or (b) quitting. And thank God, because finding another private pilot at this hour would have been a true bitch.

"You got a problem with the boss?" I asked. "Take it up with the boss. What I want to know is, are we still leaving at eight o'clock?"

"Memos don't slow down my flight check," Cooper semi-scolded in his luscious Irish accent. Oooh, European accents; I could listen to Europeans talk all day. We all sounded like illiterate bumpkins by comparison. "Gunshots don't slow down my flight check. I could tell you stories—but I can't, the government made me promise."

Cooper had first worked for Jessica's dad and, when her folks died (an ugly yet fitting death, and one I'll get into another time) and their assets transferred to her (she'd been an emancipated minor), he kept right on flying for her.

And, as he'd said, Cooper had heard things. Chances were he'd already known I was walking around dead. He was just miffed that Jessica hadn't told him a year ago.

And you know, for a decrepit fellow, he wasn't bad looking. Tall—my height—with eyes the color of new denim and a shock of pure white hair that he wore down over his shoulders, he was like an ancient hippie, one who had never touched drugs or alcohol (unnatural creature!).

He was wearing what Jessica laughingly called his uniform: khaki shorts, sandals, and a T-shirt that read "Jesus saves. He passes to Noah. Noah scores!" He had tons of weird shirts about Jesus. People picked fights. It was unreal, yet cool . . . sort of like Cooper himself.

"Okay, then." I stood, forgetting I had been sitting on the plane, and banged my head on the ceiling. "Ow!

All right, so I'll see you in another hour or so. They're, um, they're done loading Antonia and my husband's pulling together some paperwork . . ." (For what, I had no idea—Sinclair had his fingers in a lot of pies, and I wasn't interested enough to ask. He might answer, and then I'd have to listen. Or look like I was listening, which was harder than it sounded.) "Anyway, we'll be back a little later."

"I'll be ready, mum."

"And for the zillionth time: Betsy. It's Betsy."

"Whatever you say, mum."

Polite as always, he didn't turn his back on me while I scuttled out of the plane and down the stairs.

There! One unpleasant chore out of the way. Cooper knew the scoop and, even better, hadn't tried to offer me a washcloth soaked in holy water.

But I was going to have a word with my alleged best friend about her irritating memo.

I mean, jeez. Immortality didn't give me any interest in any subject not directly involving my life? Didn't she stop to think how *I* would feel if Cooper read that about me?

Not to mention *I* wasn't even cc'd on the thing!

I swear, I didn't know what had gotten into that girl since I cured her cancer and she had to dump her boyfriend because he hated my guts. Frankly, I'd been having a terrible time this week.

And now rogue memos! It was too much for anyone to expect me to handle, which I would be pointing out to her the minute I saw her . . .

Self-centered? Me? Sometimes that girl didn't know me at all.

Get to know Vampire Queen Betsy Taylor
in the *New York Times* bestselling series by

MaryJanice Davidson

Undead and Uneasy

Undead and Unpopular

Undead and Unreturnable

Undead and Unappreciated

Undead and Unwed

Undead and Unemployed

"Delightful, wicked fun!"
—*New York Times* bestselling author
Christine Feehan

"Think *Sex and the City*—only the
city is Minneapolis and it's filled
with demons and vampires."
—*Publishers Weekly*

penguin.com